Also by Natasha D. Frazier

<u>Devotionals</u>

The Life Your Spirit Craves

Not Without You

The Life Your Spirit Craves for Mommies

<u>Fiction</u>

Love, Lies & Consequences

Through Thick & Thin: Love, Lies & Consequences Book 2

Note from the Author

I am thankful to my Heavenly Father, who has allowed me the opportunity to do the thing that brings me joy and peace. He has blessed me with the heart to encourage women and the ability to do that through writing. Thank you for entrusting me with such a task. He has also given me a wonderful family who supports my writing career. Eddie, my awesome husband, I love you and appreciate you for all that you do. Thank you for your unwavering support. My babies: Eden, Ethan & Emilyn, mommy loves each of you dearly. To my mom, dad, stepdad, sisters, and extended family, I thank each of you for your love and support from afar.

To my special set of girlfriends who push me to go further and have encouraged me from the very start: Tiera, Toccara & Shenitra - I love you ladies and appreciate your friendship.

Readers - You each hold a special place in my heart. Thank you for continuing on this literary journey with me. To the 5aithful 5abulous 5ive book club, I just want to tell you that you all rock and I appreciate your support!

Much love & many blessings,

Natasha

Shattered Vows

(Love, Lies & Consequences Book 3)

NATASHA D. FRAZIER

CHAPTER 1

Dressed in only her undergarments, Chloe poised herself at her antique vanity table applying a thin layer of makeup and eyeshadow from her palette filled with hues of brown. She hardly ever wore makeup, but tonight was different. It was her and Rico's eighth wedding anniversary and she was doing her best to at least look the part of a happy wife.

They had spent the last year trying to reconcile their marriage after his affair with Raegan. Their last marriage counseling session was a month ago, and she couldn't help hearing the pastor's words replay in her mind. *Love is a choice. Staying in your marriage is a choice. Fighting for your marriage is a choice.*

God gives you strength, but what you do with that strength is up to you. Choose wisely.

Choose wisely. Is that what her husband thought he was doing when he chose Raegan? When he cheated before Raegan? She'd forgiven him before, but how was she to forgive him again? *Forgive seventy times seven,* the Word of God that she'd hidden in the deep recesses of her heart so long ago chided. *But this feels like seventy times seven plus one. How am I supposed to get through this?*

They'd spent months in counseling and things still weren't quite right. They were both trying to work past the stench of his infidelity, but their relationship was starting to feel forced, at least on her part. Fake smiles, cordial chatter and flimsy hugs. That was the extent of them touching. Sex was out of the question. Anytime her body wanted it, the feeling quickly dissipated at the thought of him being in another woman's bed. This was not the happily ever after she thought she would have. But hopefully, tonight would be different. She was turning over a new leaf. She planned to put forth her best effort during their date tonight. It almost felt like a first date since they hadn't been out in more than a year, because of her work schedule and then their issues with his extramarital affairs.

She'd chosen her outfit and carefully laid it on the bed. She would wear a camel-colored empire-waist dress that stopped just above the knee to match her newly purchased Steve Madden pumps. She primped in the mirror a while longer than needed. She was consumed by thoughts of where her marriage was headed. Was she really able to get past everything that happened? The deceit. The lies. She had to give it one more shot before calling it quits.

Chloe fingered her short curls after spraying on a touch of Rico's favorite perfume, Cashmere Mist, a part of last year's anniversary gift. She stood to get dressed, but his presence kept her from moving toward the bed. He didn't say anything and she didn't turn around, but she felt him in the room long before she smelled his Armani cologne.

Dressed in a red and brown plaid blazer, complemented with a red long-sleeved buttoned-down shirt, jeans, and loafers, Rico stood about five feet away from her drinking in her beauty with his eyes. How could he not have appreciated her before? Tonight he was hoping to change that. He was taking her to the Improv Comedy Club; that was where they went on their first date. Laughs were always good for the soul and he hoped that would get her reminiscing on how things used to be between them and how they could be that way again. Even better. They only needed to try. Harder.

He inched closer to her and placed his hands on either side of her shoulders and caressed them. He felt her stiffen under his touch and again he was disappointed. It was their anniversary, after all. He had hoped his efforts of marriage counseling, catering to all of her needs and giving her more attention than he ever thought he could give would have been enough. Instead, he constantly found himself coming up short when it came to receiving anything in return from her.

"I'll wait for you in the living room, honey," Rico said softly against her ear before caressing it with a tender kiss. He walked out of the room without waiting for a response from her.

Chloe exhaled when she heard his footsteps on the wooden stairwell. She didn't realize that she had been holding her breath ever since she felt his hands on her body. *I have to stop doing that,* she chastised herself. She knew that he was feeling rejected. But how did he think he made her feel when that woman showed up at the coffee shop carrying his child?

She pulled on her dress and fidgeted with it until she slid the zipper into position. Trying to get that zipper up had always put a strain on her arms, but she managed to get the job done alone. She slipped into her shoes and turned around in front of the mirror, giving her clothes, makeup and hair a once-over before meeting Rico downstairs.

Rico let out a low whistle as Chloe descended the stairs with her matching camel-colored clutch under her arm. She was beautiful and he made sure she knew it.

"I'm the luckiest man in the world to have you on my arm tonight. You look beautiful, sweetie," Rico complimented as he took her hand when she descended to the last three steps. When she made it to the bottom, he lifted her hand and brushed her wedding band with his fingers before planting a kiss on her hand.

"Thank you." Chloe blushed a little and returned the compliment. "You look nice, too." She noticed that he was wearing her favorite cologne as well, but didn't make mention of it. Rico placed her hand around his arm and escorted her to the car. Their drive to the Improv was filled with chatter from Rico about what they did on previous anniversaries. She didn't add much to the conversation, only nodded and smiled mostly. She had to admit that those times were nice, but this one was much different. In her mind was the insurmountable obstacle in front of them.

Rico had purchased their tickets online so they walked straight past the ticket booth to the entrance, where they were greeted by a hostess and shown to their VIP table near the stage. Noting the dim lighting, soft R&B music and the newly renovated facility, Chloe remembered their first date at the Improv, where they saw the comedian Arnez J in standup. They laughed until their stomachs and throats were in pain. She was hoping she would get another whiff of that tonight, although she didn't know who the comedian was going to be. She just knew that she could use a laugh right about now. And not just any laugh, but a magic laugh that would take away all of the pain that she was feeling and trying so hard to push aside. The type of laughter that would somehow wipe the slate clean for the two of them. She was sure there was no such thing, but she was ready for the magic she hoped the night would bring for her.

She ordered a Caesar salad and he ordered buffalo wings to enjoy before the show started. On cue, the show began when the waitress came to take away their empty plates. They were tickled a little by the warm-up acts but nothing like what she was waiting for. However, she was feeling more relaxed and her body didn't stiffen as it did earlier when Rico pulled her chair closer to his and put his arm around her.

There were still a few residual laughs from the crowd as the host appeared onstage to announce the headliner for the night—Will the Thrill. Chloe didn't recognize the comedian's stage name, so she knew she hadn't heard any of his jokes before. New material. Great.

Will the Thrill jumped straight into his routine after the round of applause subsided. His first joke was about dating and how he wasn't ready to commit to his girlfriend by getting married.

"C'mon now men. Y'all know how much extra work it is to hide the side woman when you get married. Gotta put all these codes in your phone, use aliases and lie, lie, lie. Even when you get caught, stick to the lie. Ain't that right my man?" he joked as he gestured toward Rico.

Her anticipation shaned at those jokes. In fact, they weren't funny at all. Bad choice in her mind. What began to tick her off was that Rico was doubled over in laughter . . . clearly, something he shouldn't have been laughing at given the situation they were in.

"What in the hell is so funny, Rico?" she sneered, leaning to the side to look up at him wiping tears from his eyes.

"What?" Rico asked, clearly confused.

"So cheating is funny?"

"Sweetie, these are just jokes. C'mon now."

"I'm glad you think ruining our marriage and our lives is funny. I'm getting out of here!" Chloe scooted away from the table, snatched her purse and walked away with Rico following close behind.

"Looks like someone got caught doing what I just said not to do!" the comedian joked to their retreating backs as they exited the room, causing an uproar in the crowd.

Rico grabbed her hand and she spun around. She yanked her hand back and folded her arms across her chest. The look she gave would have killed him if looks could kill. Infidelity was a sore spot with her and definitely not a laughing matter. Rico couldn't understand why she took it so seriously. Everyone in the room, except her, knew that those were only jokes. There was no reason to get upset over nothing. But to Chloe it wasn't *nothing;* it was the reason her life was turned upside down.

CHAPTER 2

Nearly two weeks had gone by since their anniversary-date disaster, and Chloe had thought more and more about the state of their relationship. It seemed as if Rico was the only one who had moved past his infidelity. He admitted he cheated and gave up his parental rights to his child, but he seemed to want to act as though it had never happened. He had never expressed remorse, and he hadn't given any promise it would never happen again or made any plans to act differently in the future. He just wanted to forget about it, and have her do so too. As for her, she had a long way to go, if she were to ever get past their issues. She'd tried and she just wasn't ready.

"Rico, I don't love you," Chloe confessed with a duffle bag slain across one shoulder and another latched onto her rolling suitcase. And she silently added, *not the way that a wife should.* She knew that she promised to love him forever on their wedding day, but he was the one who forgot or at least chose to neglect the promise he made to her. And for that, she felt like she rightfully had a reason to end their marriage. Truth be told, it was over the moment he started seeing other women. And if there was any salvaging their marriage, that notion was over when he impregnated Raegan.

"Y-you c-c-can't be s-serious," Rico stammered, lifting his head from his palms to see his wife walking toward the door with her luggage.

Chloe paused mid-stride, astonished that Rico found it surprising that she was leaving. Although Raegan lost Rico's baby, there were so many other reasons why she and Rico could not be together. No trust. No love. Only lies.

Rico raced over to her and placed his hands on the luggage handle. She had to give him another chance to make this right.

"Please don't go; I know we can work this out, baby, please. Just please give us another chance . . . please." His voice was beginning to strain as he fought to choke back the tears and the wave of emotion that threatened to overtake him, as the reality of their situation set in. She was about to leave him.

Turning slightly to face him, Chloe glared, her eyes cold. "It's funny that you think of this now. Where was all of this passion for our relationship when you were with another woman?" Chloe dared him to answer.

Rico remained silent with his hands holding her luggage. He knew there was no answer that he could give right now that would right this wrong.

"See there? That's exactly what I thought. Please remove your hands from my luggage or be helpful and put it in the trunk," Chloe snarled. She glanced down at her suitcase as if she had some sort of superpower to remove his hands.

Rico dropped his hands from the handle and Chloe opened one of his hands to place her keys inside. He was a gentleman by all means, but there was no way he was going to stand there and help his wife leave him.

Without another word, Chloe shifted the luggage so that she wouldn't drop anything, opened the door and went to her car. Rico had to try once more, so he followed her through the front door to the driveway.

"Where are you going?" Rico pleaded.

"Never mind that; I will be back for the rest of my things at a later time. Please do *not* contact me. I really just need to be away from you."

"For how long?" Rico asked, hoping that her need to get away was temporary.

"I can't say whether it's a week, a month or forever. . . . I just need some time." Saying those words out loud brought her some relief. She had to break free.

Rico felt defeated. He stood there with his head low, shoulders slumped, hands in pockets, watching as his wife packed her things into her car to possibly leave his life forever.

Chloe watched Rico in the rearview mirror as she drove off. Her heart broke for him as she saw him standing in the driveway. He looked dejected. However, the sadness she felt for him did nothing for the heartbreak she was experiencing. For the life of her, she just couldn't understand how he could do something like that to her, after all they had gone through. She had always been there for him and made sure she gave him special attention when she wasn't at work.

She was planning to spend a few weeks with a friend before she rented an apartment, but she got the feeling that she really needed to get away. Away from Houston. As far away from Rico as possible so that she could think.

She'd only told him she didn't love him to hurt his feelings. Although she couldn't say without a shadow of a doubt that she didn't love him, she also couldn't say that she still loved him. She was caught somewhere in between.

Rico stood in the driveway for thirty minutes hoping that Chloe would turn the car around, but she never did. The words of his friend Michael suddenly echoed in his mind. All of his dirt was finally catching up with him and he had no one to blame but himself.

"Lord, I know You haven't heard from me in a while," Rico began to pray as he slowly walked back into the empty house. "But I need You to bring my wife back. I know I've done some terrible things to her and I've already apologized; I just don't know what else to do. How can I get her back? I've really messed up this time, God, and only You can help me through this. Please Lord. Amen," Rico ended his prayer the moment he stepped inside the house. He closed the door and slid down on the floor against it, praying again, this time silently.

His prayer was interrupted by someone knocking on his front door. He quickly jumped up and flung the door open, thinking that God must have answered his prayers and Chloe was back. It was only the mailman dropping off a package that couldn't fit into their mailbox. He reclaimed his spot on the floor against the door, rubbing his hands behind his head. *What am I going to do?*

CHAPTER 3

Rico visited his home church—a place he hadn't been in quite some time. In fact, he hadn't been to church in a couple of years, aside from the time he visited Raegan's church. When Chloe's work schedule started to prevent them from going to Sunday worship services together, he didn't go at all, though he watched the services online from time to time. But eventually, he hardly ever made time to do even that.

Rico mindlessly went through the motions of the church service that morning. Standing when instructed to stand, greeting his neighbor when solicited, holding a hand during prayer and returning a hug with a pretend smile plastered across his face. He couldn't fully give himself over to worship when the choir sang because he was preoccupied with his wife leaving him. He completely missed the announcements and altar call for prayer and heard only bits and pieces of the pastor's sermon, even though it was on the topic of adultery.

When the service ended, he greeted fellow church members who had been sitting near him. After spending several minutes catching up with a young couple who mentioned that they hadn't seen him in a while, he returned to his seat, watching several couples who had smiles plastered across their faces, appearing to be happy, with their children bobbing alongside them.

Even with the hundreds of parishioners in the sanctuary, he still felt alone. The hugs and smiles did nothing to help ease the anxiety he felt about the future of his marriage. Why couldn't he and Chloe be happy like most of the other church members seemed to be? He had no idea where things went wrong or when he decided that it was okay to step out on his wife. Now she was gone and he was likely never going to get her back.

He wasn't well versed in the Bible but he did know that his adultery was an acceptable reason for Chloe to get a divorce. Adultery. Such a dirty word when he thought about it. He had become an adulterer, risking everything for temporary pleasure.

The church cleared. The pastor entered the sanctuary to walk along the pews and pray for the church and its members as he did every week before and after service. Noticing Rico sitting there, he walked over to him to make sure everything was okay.

"Son, are you all right? Is there something I can help you with?" Pastor Lewis asked, peering over his bifocals.

"I'm not sure," Rico answered hesitantly. He glanced up at Pastor Lewis but quickly diverted his attention in the opposite direction for fear that the pastor would be able to see right through him.

Pastor Lewis sat down on the pew in front of Rico and eyed him carefully. He silently prayed for discernment and help from God for the young man. With a congregation of more than a thousand members, he didn't know Rico personally, but could see that his spirit was troubled.

"What's disturbing you? No way you'd be sitting here if nothing was bothering you. Most of the saints head straight to a restaurant or home for Sunday dinner when service is over. Might I ask why you aren't doing the same?"

"I have no one to do any of that with." Rico shrugged, avoiding eye contact.

Pastor Lewis noticed the wedding band on Rico's hand and lifted it.

"And why is that?"

"You don't have time to hear this today, Pastor," Rico admitted shamefully. He was beginning to think it was a bad idea to stay behind, but he had nowhere else to turn.

Pastor Lewis shifted in his seat.

"Well, my wife is getting our children ready so that we can all get something to eat, but I do have a few minutes, especially when I can clearly see that someone is hurting."

"Chloe, my wife . . . she's gone," Rico said, his eyes becoming watery at the mere thought of going home to an empty house. The pastor nodded for Rico to continue. "That adulterer you spoke of in your sermon today, that's me. I cheated on her and got another woman pregnant. The other woman actually lost the baby but that doesn't change what I did," Rico confessed. He rubbed his hands along his pant leg, trying to hide his shame and relieve the pain in his heart.

"So what do I do, Pastor?" Rico asked after a long moment of silence. He knew that Pastor Lewis couldn't necessarily give him a precise answer to get her back, but he figured it was worth a try.

"I tell you what, come see me in my office tomorrow. This is going to take much longer than a two-minute conversation," Pastor Lewis responded after eyeing Rico carefully for several seconds. "What time works best for you?"

"Are you here tomorrow evening? I can come when I get off work," said Rico. Seeing the pastor one on one would never have been on his agenda, but he was desperate. If the pastor could give him any kind of advice that would get him remotely close to getting his wife back, seeing him was worth the shot.

∞

Every time Chloe saw a pregnant woman in the hospital, it pushed her thoughts back to her husband—and another woman carrying his baby. She needed to take a leave of absence much sooner than she'd planned. Away from the city. Away from Rico. Away from anything that reminded her of his indiscretions.

One of Chloe's co-workers walked up to her and nudged her shoulders.

"Hey you! Why are you sulking around here? Have you forgotten that you work in a hospital and patients need to see a smiling nurse?" her nurse friend teased.

"I know. I'm dealing with a few personal things. I'm getting things in order so that I can take some time off and return with that smile that our patients need to see," Chloe tossed over her shoulder, as she shuffled a few files on the counter.

"Atta girl!" Her friend nudged her shoulders again and walked off.

Chloe completed her paperwork to take a leave of absence; the plan was to take three months off to return home to Tennessee. She'd discussed the leave of absence with her boss right after the affair and had gone through the process to get approval, but held on to the paperwork until she decided that taking time away was the right thing to do. And now, staying didn't seem to be an option since her marriage seemed irreparable. She said a silent prayer before walking into her boss' office to hand over the paperwork. Relief washed over her as she cleaned out her locker and headed to her packed car.

"What's this I hear about you leaving?"

Chloe spun around a few steps away from her car door to see Terry, a fellow nurse, calling to her from across the parking garage. Chloe placed a short strand of hair behind her ear as she peered up at him and considered his question, trying to decide what kind of information he was fishing for.

"Yeah I am. I have way too many unused vacation days. I need to get away for a while," responded Chloe.

"A while can be a very long time. How long are we talking about here?"

"A month or so maybe?" Chloe told a half-truth.

"Month? Seriously? Well, have lunch with me before you go. Surely you can spare an hour before you jump ship."

Chloe checked her watch, then agreed; she hopped in her car to meet Terry at a nearby Mexican restaurant. With the cloudiness that filled her head, she wondered if meeting him was the best idea. Terry had once made it known that he found her attractive, and when she informed him that she was married, he backed off. So she wondered what this was all about. Perhaps he really wanted to have a friendly lunch.

Chloe and Terry placed their orders at the counter and took their seats.

"Tell me what's really going on, Chloe. We've worked together for nearly five years and this isn't like you. I've been watching you for the past couple of weeks and something just hasn't been right with you."

Chloe sipped her water and eyed him intently.

"Completely off the record, I swear." Terry held up his hands as if to surrender.

"It's like I said, I just need some time away."

Terry shifted in his seat and sat up straight. "I know this is none of my business, but my ex-wife made the mistake of running when things went wrong in our marriage. It didn't help the matter and it drove us apart even more. If Rico is the reason you're running, rethink your decision. If you even think there's a small chance that you want to work on your marriage, stay. Don't leave. It won't help the situation, trust me," Terry advised before biting a tortilla chip.

Chloe gave a weak smile. She neither confirmed nor denied that Rico was the reason she was leaving. Instead, she briefly considered Terry's words. He was an objective person, but she knew herself and knew she needed the time away.

"Thanks Terry. You're such a wise man. Who would have thought," she teased, munching on the tortilla chips as well.

Throughout lunch, Terry continuously tried to slide bits and pieces of advice to Chloe, even though he wasn't completely sure why she was taking so much time off. However, he was confident enough to know that someone so dedicated to her profession wouldn't pack up and leave her job for a while unless it was relationship related. She would have mentioned it if a family member was sick or something. He couldn't imagine anything else that would have her acting so strangely.

CHAPTER 4

I don't love you. The words echoed in Chloe's head as she allowed the wind to kiss her face. She could have taken a flight to Tennessee, but the drive was what she needed. Time to clear her mind. Think. Allow the whispers of the Holy Spirit to give her guidance. She only stopped to refill her gas tank and to buy snacks along the route. She wasn't in any rush to get to Nashville, but she needed to be as far away from Houston and Rico's lies as possible.

She loved Rico but she hated what he did to her and their marriage, and she wasn't sure that she could get over it. Certainly couples work through that type of thing all the time—but could she and Rico? She wouldn't be able to trust him ever again. She didn't want to be at work worried about what he was doing and who he was doing it with. She didn't want to be the type of wife who questioned her husband's every move, checked his cell phone call log and messages, or hacked into his e-mail accounts. That would drive both of them crazy. She swore that she wouldn't live that way. Ever.

She knew what the Bible said about marriage, and if she interpreted it correctly, since he committed adultery she could divorce him and God wouldn't hold it against her. Her demanding career had been in the way of her going to church, but she often prayed, studied her Bible and read devotionals when she could. Was it something that she did wrong to deserve that treatment from her husband? Was she being punished for something she was unaware of?

The nearly twelve-and-a-half-hour drive ended when she arrived on her sister's doorpost. It was almost one o'clock in the morning, so she stooped down to retrieve the spare key from a fake plant near the front door. She was surprised when she walked inside and saw her sister sitting on the couch wrapped in a purple robe, sipping tea, as if she'd been waiting up for a teenager who stayed out past curfew.

"Kelly! Why on earth are you up at this hour?"

"Waiting on you! Duh! It's not like I could fall asleep anyway, knowing that you were on the road all by yourself." Kelly placed her mug on the coffee table and ran over to greet her sister. "Besides, I know you're tired from the drive but I needed to talk to you and make sure you're okay before I could go to bed. Some of us still have jobs to go to, you know?" Kelly reminded Chloe as they walked arm in arm to the sofa. "Sit here, I'll be right back with a cup of tea for you," said Kelly as she walked to the kitchen to make her sister a cup of chai tea so they could have a sisterly discussion.

"You really don't have to make anything for me; I'm fine," Chloe called over her shoulder to her sister as she plopped down on the couch, kicked off her flats and waited for her to return. She knew that Kelly wouldn't listen to her; she never did. Given that Chloe was the older sister, she figured she could boss Kelly around a little but it never worked. Kelly had always been strong willed.

"Here you go! Nice and warm. I added a bit of 2 percent milk to it. I promise it tastes a lot better that way," said Kelly as she sat down next to her sister and took a sip of her own tea. Seeing as though there was no way around the awkwardness surrounding the reason that Chloe was at her home on a whim, without Rico, Kelly allowed a moment to pass before she asked the inevitable.

"So is it really over?"

"I don't know when my life changed," Chloe whispered, taking another sip of tea to gather her thoughts. She'd gone through the situation a million times in her head on her drive there, but she still couldn't grasp what Rico had been thinking. "His cheating . . . I just can't get over it."

"So what was the final straw? What happened?"

Chloe kept trying to make sense of it all by rehashing the details of Rico's affair and how she found out about it, as if it was her first time telling it to Kelly. She was never one to go through his personal things, and she usually didn't answer his phone but that particular day, she did. She wasn't sure what led her to do it. Besides, the caller ID displayed *Raymond*. How was she to know that it would actually be Raegan?

Chloe talked about her meeting with Raegan at the coffee shop, finding out about the baby and bringing Rico in the middle of it to confirm everything. Although Chloe had already told her sister about the affair, she never revealed that there was a baby involved. Now that her marriage was practically over, there was no need to hold back any of the disgusting details. "I never thought I would be the wife asking another woman about my husband. Never thought it. Never even dreamed that this would happen to me. I keep replaying the situation over and over again in my mind, trying to figure out if there was something I did wrong. Something I did to push him away . . ." Chloe's words trailed off as Kelly interrupted her.

"Hold on big sis! Now that is one thing that I don't want you to do—blame yourself. Rico made a series of choices that led him to his indiscretions. We both know that." Kelly's blood was boiling at the audacity of Rico. She had other choice words to say about him but kept her composure and remained the listening ear.

She was certain that Chloe didn't need her to say how *no good* he was, and she definitely didn't want to say anything that would affect Chloe's decision to stay or go.

"Yeah, but still . . . I can't help but wonder what he must have been thinking," Chloe said.

"So is Rico planning to be in the baby's life? How is that going to work out?"

Chloe closed her eyes remembering the incident. She had left out that one detail. She then shared with her sister that Raegan was involved in a car accident shortly after their meeting and lost the baby. Her heart broke for Raegan. Although she didn't like the circumstances, she didn't wish her any harm.

"Oh no," Kelly said quietly. She silently thanked God for her two small children sleeping upstairs. As a mother, she knew that had to be difficult for the other woman.

"So what now?"

"If you were me, what would you do?" Chloe asked pointedly. *What kind of question was that?* Kelly had to stop and think. *What am I supposed to say or do?*

Kelly bit her tongue and shrugged her shoulders. Her husband was thousands of miles away overseas, serving his country. She didn't know how she would respond in such a situation. Her motto had always been, *Divorce is not an option,* but she always prayed that nothing would ever happen to make her have to put that motto to the test. Nothing such as what her sister was going through. She always felt like she could handle anything but infidelity, and she was quite certain her sister felt the same way. Ultimate betrayal.

"Doesn't the Bible give me a pass to end this marriage since he cheated?" Chloe mentioned.

"Is that what the Bible says?"

"Don't quote me on it but I'm pretty sure that's true. I will find the verse for you—well, for me—tomorrow," Chloe said as she leaned back and rested her head against the sofa pillows.

"Do you want to leave? Can you honestly see yourself without him? Are you better off without him? Do you want to be single again?"

Therein lay the problem for Chloe. Rico was her husband and she felt like she'd done all that she could do by going to counseling. But at what point should she throw in the towel? She couldn't picture staying with him, though she couldn't fathom being without him. He was the one she chose to spend the rest of her life with; there wasn't supposed to be a second go round.

"Kelly, I just don't think things will ever be the same between us. I don't know if I can leave, but I know that I can't stay," Chloe cried, releasing the tears that she'd been holding in for weeks.

Kelly placed her mug back on the coffee table and held her sister, encouraging her to let it all out. She was the baby sister so she had no rank, but she would do her best to encourage her sister in whatever way possible to help her heal. Should Chloe give her marriage another chance? Kelly didn't have the answer to that, but she wanted her sister to be at peace with whatever decision she made.

Kelly silently prayed. *Father in Heaven, my heart hurts for my sister. I know she is in pain, facing something that she never thought she'd have to deal with. I pray that You give her a peace that surpasses all understanding in this situation. I know this is not an easy situation to deal with and will be a long process, but I pray that You give her strength to make it to the other side. And whatever You need me to do to help, I am Your vessel, so help me to put aside my personal feelings in this situation so that I may honor You. In Jesus' name, Amen.*

CHAPTER 5

Rico sat in the pastor's study. Framed Scriptures and spiritually themed decorative items held his attention while he waited for Pastor Lewis to end his phone call. His eyes rested on a gold-colored name plate on the pastor's desk with the words *I can do all things through Christ which strengthens me* inscribed on it instead of the pastor's name.

All things? He wondered if that Scripture could prove to be true for him in his current situation. Would Christ give him what he needed to get his wife back? Did *all things* apply in this situation? Or did that only apply to spiritual things? Would the pastor give him some words of encouragement—something good enough to win Chloe's love back? She said that she no longer loved him.

"Pardon me. That call lasted a bit longer than I thought it would," Pastor Lewis commented as he replaced the receiver. "Tell me why you're here," Pastor Lewis demanded as he rested his shoulders back in his leather chair.

Okay, now this is unbelievable. Wasn't he the one who asked me to come see him? Rico wondered and considered the question. Was it a trick question? He thought for a moment before responding because he hadn't thought much about why he was coming—only that he was desperate and hoped that Pastor Lewis could give him some Scripture that he could at least quote to Chloe to make her believe that her leaving him wasn't the right thing to do.

"I want my wife back," Rico said after careful contemplation of his question.

"Umm hmm. Well seeking direction from God is definitely the best start, but much is going to be required of you; so let's start from the beginning. Tell me what happened. What is it that brought you to this place? Your wife leaving you and all. And please tell the entire truth. These sessions will only work if you're honest," Pastor Lewis reminded Rico.

Rico leaned back in his seat, blew out a chestful of pent-up air, rubbed his hands along his pants and thought for a moment.

Sessions? Plural? He had been hopeful that he would get his answer today, but he was more than desperate, so he was willing to do everything it would take to start anew with his wife.

"Long story short, I met this woman who was absolutely breathtaking. I took her out a few times, talked to her on the phone repeatedly and I began to fall for her. She seemed so perfect. When I realized what I was getting myself into, I ended it. But I guess it was too late because she ended up pregnant with my baby," Rico shared shamefully.

Pastor Lewis studied him for a moment. He noticed Rico's eyes were lit up when speaking of this woman and that concerned him. He jotted down some notes on a pad.

"What compelled you to start seeing her even though you were married?"

"Man, I mean, sir, I don't even know. It was never supposed to go so far. It was casual at first, but she became serious."

"Wait one moment. I am a pastor but I'm also a man. So you and I both know that if she was becoming serious, you were giving her a reason to be. Did you tell her you loved her? That you would leave your wife and marry her? What was it?"

Rico shook his head at the thought of everything he'd told Raegan. It felt awkward to share those things with the pastor. Actually telling someone everything he did made him feel dirty, because he knew he was wrong. He didn't want the pastor to think of him as some dirty womanizer, because that wasn't who he was. He was just a guy who got caught up in the moment, in his opinion.

"She didn't know I was married; I never told her," Rico admitted, averting his eyes from the pastor's gaze. He didn't want to see the look on his face. He was certain it would be disapproving. "Like I said, it was never supposed to go that far. I told her I loved her and that I could see us having a future together," Rico told a half-truth. He felt terrible about lying to the pastor, but he couldn't bring himself to say that he told Raegan that she would one day be his wife when he was already married.

Pastor Lewis had had these types of sessions many times and he knew that Rico wasn't being completely honest with him.

"So how did she find out you were married? How did your wife find out about her?" Pastor Lewis continued to question. Not much of that was important, but he wanted to see just how honest Rico would be and how serious he was about getting his wife back.

"I left my phone at home one day when she called. My wife answered it. I had her name saved under an alias," Rico recounted. The more he talked about it, the worse it sounded. If he were in Chloe's shoes, he didn't know if he would take him back.

"The baby?"

"She lost the baby but before she did, I signed over my parental rights, hoping that would help smooth things over with Chloe. Hoping we could get past it," Rico explained, remembering the pain both from signing over his rights and his wife telling him that the baby didn't make it.

Pastor Lewis placed his pen on the notepad, locked his fingers together and rested his forehead against them for a moment. His head was starting to hurt from the drama that Rico had in his life. He took a moment to silently pray for guidance. When he finished, he rested his clasped hands on his desk.

"Tell me this. What was it you felt was missing in your marriage that you had to seek companionship elsewhere?"

Rico could have talked about the fact that Chloe worked a lot and attempted to shift the blame to her being away, but that wasn't it. The fact that Chloe wasn't there gave him the opportunity. He could have admired Raegan from afar and kept moving. He didn't have to seek her out on Facebook. He didn't have to ask her out. He wasn't sure why he did it, and he told the pastor so. What he needed now was for the pastor to tell him how to fix it and to stop asking all of these questions.

"I don't mean no harm, Pastor, but I need you to tell me how to get my wife back. Don't you have some type of Scripture in your arsenal for situations like this?" Rico got straight to the point. He felt like he was getting nowhere fast with the pastor's line of questioning.

"Son, what you need is Jesus."

I did not come here to hear that, sir. You have got to be kidding me. Did I just waste the last hour? Rico thought. But aloud he said, "I am already saved. What do you mean?"

Pastor Lewis handed Rico a sheet of paper with three points. The first point listed several Scriptures he suggested Rico study regarding love and marriage. The second suggestion was to write down why he cheated, and the third was to write down why he wanted his wife back. Rico glanced down at the sheet of paper. His nose flared from the anger he now felt. He could not believe that he sat in the pastor's office for an hour just to walk away with a sheet of paper that had no suggestions on what he could do to get his wife back. He wanted to crumple the paper in front of the pastor and toss it back on his desk, but that was rude. He felt like God was already disappointed with him about how he treated his wife; he couldn't have God upset with him about disrespecting the pastor as well. Instead, he folded the paper and placed it in his pocket.

"Thank you, sir. Have a good day," Rico mumbled as he walked out of the office and out of the church back to his car. He could have come up with that on his own. He sat behind the steering wheel and read the paper again. "Stupid," Rico said as he crumpled the paper and tossed it in the passenger seat. He decided that he would call his best friend, Michael. Surely he would have some decent advice for him. After all, Michael was the one who advised against seeing Raegan in the first place; he had to have some advice for him on how to get Chloe back. Something way better than those things the old pastor wrote down on that sheet of paper.

CHAPTER 6

"Does your First Lady preach often?" Chloe asked her sister Kelly as they walked back to Chloe's car after Bible study.

"About once a month. Why? Was the Spirit speaking to you through her tonight?" Kelly teased as she rubbed her shoulders against Chloe.

"I think so. Something about the last part of her sermon resonated with me. Although the message had nothing to do with marriage, ending her sermon with 1 John 4:12, talking about loving one another, made me think of Rico." She figured it was probably because she told him that she didn't love him anymore. But she didn't mean it in that way, she meant it in a romantic sort of way and that isn't what the Scripture was talking about, she mused, trying to make sense of why he popped into her mind. Her nose twitched at the thought of him.

The flashing blue and white lights in Chloe's rearview mirror brought her thoughts back from the sermon. She slowed down and pulled over to the curb. She inwardly cursed Rico; this would not be happening either had he not cheated.

Without looking at the officer, she dangled her license, registration, and car insurance documents out of the window to hand to the officer before he could even ask. She wasn't in any mood to hear, *Do you know why I pulled you over?*

Before Officer Shane McDaniels could speak, he saw that the driver held out the necessary information so that he could run her information. He peered through the window and asked if she knew why he pulled her over. She simply nodded. The sun had already set, so it was hard to make out her face. He shined his flashlight over the license and his heart nearly stopped.

"Chloe? Chloe from Old Brook Manor neighborhood?? What are you doing here?" he asked, bending over to look in the car.

The familiar voice sent a jolt through her heart that caused her to straighten in her seat. Chloe dropped her hand from her forehead and leaned on the steering wheel to get a glimpse of the face behind the voice. Just as she suspected.

"Shane? I mean Officer Shane?" She stumbled over her words a bit.

He opened the car door and Chloe jumped out to greet him. Their parents were neighbors so they practically grew up together. They lost contact with each other when Chloe moved away for college.

"How have you been, girl? You're just as gorgeous as the day you left! You know that, right?"

"Thank you. You're not too bad yourself." Chloe tried hard to hide the smile threatening to erupt from his compliments. "So does this mean you're not going to write me a ticket? Old pal?" Chloe grinned, showing nearly every tooth in her mouth, hoping that their history would keep him from writing the ticket.

"That depends on how long you're here and if you promise to meet me for dinner," Shane said, tapping the documents she had handed to him.

"Is that a bribe, Officer McDaniels?" Chloe said teasingly as she fingered the badge on his uniform shirt. Her entire demeanor had changed. She went from being annoyed to relieved. Probably more like excited. It had been quite some time since she'd had any contact with Shane.

"Call it what you want. Dinner or a ticket?" he asked and chuckled, holding up his writing pad. He sported a huge smile.

Luckily for him, it was dark enough to mask just how excited he was to see her again.

"Dinner it is. Call me tomorrow," she said as she scribbled her number on his pad and held out her hand for her insurance, registration, and license.

Shane nodded and opened the door for her and made sure she was safely inside. After saying hello to Kelly, he cautioned Chloe against speeding before walking back to his patrol car.

Kelly had been sitting in the car with her arms folded watching the exchange. She couldn't believe how her sister was acting—like she wasn't married.

"What?" Chloe studied the frown on her sister's face as she buckled her seatbelt and started the car again.

"I think you know what. Shane McDaniels is single and you're married. Isn't this the issue you're having with Rico?" Kelly reminded her.

"It's just dinner. Besides, Shane and I are old friends. He's practically like my brother. We grew up together. Remember?"

"Tell me you're not that naïve. You know that Shane has been in love with you since the beginning of time."

"He has not! And if he has, what does that have to do with anything?" Chloe retorted.

"I saw the way you were looking at him. You're married—remember? How quickly we forget."

Chloe never considered taking things past the friendship stage with Shane because that was all it had ever been with him. Friendship. There was that one time that things got out of hand, but no one knew about that other than Shane and Chloe.

"You're still married," Kelly reminded her again.

"Barely! Besides, if Rico and I were on speaking terms, I would have no problem telling him that I ran into an old friend and we were planning to have dinner. I have nothing to hide." Chloe shrugged.

Kelly shook her head and rolled her eyes heavenward. She could see this getting complicated really fast. This could be the perfect opportunity for Shane to make a move on Chloe. She was vulnerable; she needed to be loved and Rico wasn't cutting it at the moment. Having a fling with Shane would be just the thing that would make her sister think that the grass was greener on the other side. And why wouldn't it be at this point? Shane didn't cheat on her; Rico did. But since Chloe wasn't divorced, Shane was the only one with everything to lose—his heart.

CHAPTER 7

Every sad love song that Rico had ever known played on the radio on his drive home from church. Usually, he would have changed the station but the lyrics resonated with him. It was as if they were all singing about him and his mistakes.

The songs on the radio coupled with the session he'd just had with his pastor left him feeling slightly depressed. What was he going to do now? He had no idea what he would do to get Chloe back. He was planning to go home and call Michael but found himself pulling into a parking space at Memorial Herman Park. It was a beautiful day outside and he hoped that the weather would do something to raise his spirits because he was feeling pretty low.

He got out of the car and changed into a pair of sneakers that he kept in his trunk. Going for a run might do the trick. Something about the wind hitting his face and music blasting in his ears always helped to clear his mind. Perhaps he could get some clarity by spending some time alone in the sanctity of God's creation.

After shoving his headphones into his ears and switching his iPod to something that would get him in the mood for exercise, his steps became one with the concrete trail. Before long, he'd run two and a half miles, sweat dripping along his face that he didn't bother to wipe off. The depths of his problems made him want to press even harder and go even farther until the sight of something beautiful forced him to pause: a very pregnant Raegan and a stroller.

I thought she lost the baby, he pondered. He slowed his steps as he neared her. For a moment, he thought his eyes were playing tricks on him, but he would know those glistening curls anywhere. Though he was trying to catch his breath from the run, his heart would not cooperate. As he drew closer, she still didn't notice him, but allowed himself to wonder if it was possible to see a face that resembled his inside the stroller. *What if she didn't lose the baby?*

"Raegan?" His voice was cracked. He hadn't laid eyes on her since the day in the coffee shop where he signed over his parental rights to their unborn child.

Raegan's body stiffened at the sound of his voice—the voice she associated with betrayal, lies and deception. She had hoped she'd never see him again but figured she wouldn't be so lucky. She was sitting on the park bench, leaning over a stroller.

"Rico" was the only word she allowed to flow from her lips, without making a move to look at him. Her attention remained focused on folding a blanket and tossing toys into the basket underneath the stroller. Maybe she was being petty, but nothing other than heartache arose from her knowing him, and she didn't see a need to entertain him any further.

"If I could take it all back, I would. The hurt and the pain I caused you, I mean." He wanted to add, "If I could have been there for you through the loss of our child I would have," but now he was no longer sure what was going on. Did Chloe lie to get back at him for his indiscretions? His head was starting to pound as he tried to figure out what was going on.

Why does she have a stroller? If she didn't lose the baby, how old would the baby be? Rico silently tried to reason and do a quick calculation in his head.

He continued without any indication that she was even listening, "I did care about you and I never wanted you to get hurt—" Rico began to apologize. Raegan paused for a moment, but she didn't acknowledge his comment. Seeing that his words didn't seem to have an effect on Raegan, he stopped. Why was he apologizing? Wasn't it all over? It had been nearly a year now. Had she let it go?

The moment became even more awkward for Rico when Caleb approached carrying their son Nicholas, who was adopted by Raegan shortly after he came to live with them. He had taken Nicholas to get ice cream from the truck that circled the park playing music, capturing all the kids' attention. He leaned over to kiss Raegan, who had been rubbing her protruding belly when he returned.

"Are you all right babe?" he asked, placing his palm on top of hers, not even acknowledging Rico's presence.

"Oh, I'm sorry man," Rico found himself apologizing again, holding his palms up in surrender. He didn't want any trouble and didn't want Caleb to think that he was trying to make a move on his wife. "Beautiful family. Glad you all are doing well," Rico said finally as he backed away. He jammed his headphones back into his ears and continued his run, this time running even faster than before.

A small child? What happened? And married to Caleb? He knew Caleb had a thing for her simply by the way he said her name that day they were all together in Buffalo Wild Wings. Apparently what they had before Rico got involved with Raegan was way more serious than she let on. A tinge of jealousy swept through his heart. Raegan and Caleb had everything he wanted but couldn't have, especially not at this moment. But who was he to be jealous?

Had he never begun seeing Raegan in the first place, he wouldn't be in this predicament. Rico's thoughts swirled around in his head at the same pace as his feet pounded the pavement.

Another two and a half miles behind him and he found himself back in the area near his car. It took just fifteen minutes for the last stretch. He ran over to his car and rested his head against the hood, trying to steady his breathing and his thoughts. Once he regained control, he called Michael. Although he thought he knew what his best friend would say, he was hoping that Michael could give him a little insight.

"What's up, man? You've been mighty quiet over there. What's been going on?" Michael's voice boomed through the line.

"Been trying to patch things up with Chloe since the whole Raegan thing, man. It's not working. She left."

"So what are you going to do about it?"

"That's why I was calling you. You're good at this kind of stuff . . . being a good husband and all. Can you give a brother some tips?"

"I think I gave you my best tip some time ago. Do you remember what that was? To leave that other woman alone," Michael answered his own question.

Rico knew that was coming but that didn't help him now. He needed something new. Something fresh. Something that would make Chloe understand that he still loved her and he wanted to be her husband. He was all in this time and he needed her to believe him and to want to be with him again too.

Rico slid into the car and just sat there. He didn't bother to start the car because he didn't know where he was headed. He didn't want to go home again to a cold, empty, lonely house.

"Well, we know I didn't listen then, but I'm listening now."

"I don't think you'll like what I'm going to say."

"Try me," Rico said. He was desperate. How come no one could see that?

"You need counseling. What made you cheat in the first place? Whatever the issue is, it needs to be addressed and taken care of or else it just might happen again and you'll be making this phone call to me again in a couple of years."

Rico grunted. He recalled his earlier session with Pastor Lewis and shared the details with Michael. It seemed as though Michael agreed with the pastor. Rico didn't like it, but if two happily married men shared the same advice, he reluctantly decided that he would at least give it a shot.

"I don't see how this is going to help, but I'll give it a try," Rico agreed as he picked up the crumpled piece of paper Pastor Lewis had given him with further instructions.

"If you want Chloe back, you're gonna have to do the work, man. It's as simple as that," Michael reminded him.

Rico knew Michael was right. He promised himself that he would do whatever it took, and it seemed as if his first steps were to follow Pastor Lewis' advice and to continue the counseling sessions, as much as he didn't want to. His desire to keep his marriage was greater than his thoughts regarding this assignment, so he planned to try harder. He was ready to renew his commitment to Chloe and his marriage like never before.

CHAPTER 8

Chloe met Shane at Arnold's Country Kitchen. According to Shane, Arnold's served the best Southern soul food in the city. He made it a point to stop by at least once a month to get his fill of soul food. On a normal day, he stuck with grilled meat and veggies.

Shane held the door as Chloe walked into the bright red building. Her nostrils were immediately filled with the smell of fried green tomatoes. She moaned at the thought of tasting them. She hadn't eaten those in years.

They walked to the counter and silently read over the menu for several moments. Shane knew what he wanted, so he stole sideways glances at Chloe while she perused the blackboard filled with menu items. *Hands down, the best traffic violation stop I've ever made,* he thought.

"So what are you going to order?" Chloe asked as she inched forward to place her order, breaking Shane's train of thought.

"Turnip greens, fried chicken, cornbread. I'm generally a healthy eater but I have to satisfy my taste buds every once in a while. You really can't go wrong with anything you order," he spoke over his shoulder so that she could hear him. She stood at least a foot and a half shorter than him.

"Hmm. Okay." They placed their orders, grabbed their trays filled with food and found a table. They arrived at just the right time because the crowd was filling in behind them.

After saying a quick prayer, Shane allowed her a moment to taste her food before getting into her business. As far as he knew, she was married. Where was her wedding band? Where was her husband?

"These fried green tomatoes are to die for!" She relished the flavor of the well-seasoned, crispy vegetable.

"Told ya! Say, what brings you back to this neck of the woods? You were the last person I expected to pull over." He chuckled at the thought of Chloe speeding since he had always known her as a goody two shoes.

"Visiting my sister. I needed to get away. Things have been crazy back in Houston for a while now."

Shane noticed the shadow on her left ring finger that obviously housed her wedding band. Even though they had grown up relatively close, he didn't want to overstep his bounds and ask her directly if the craziness in Houston had to do with her husband. He remembered his heart tearing into pieces when she said *I do.*

"Yep, it's about Rico," Chloe confirmed when she saw Shane eyeballing her ring finger. "He cheated," she said, shrugging her shoulders, before taking another bite of food.

Shane could say the polite *I'm sorry to hear that,* but he wasn't sorry. Sorry it happened to her, yes. But sorry that she could possibly be free again, definitely not. This could be *his* chance to wife her up. He knew things wouldn't happen quickly, but now there was hope. Only once had he told her how he felt and since it was in the heat of the moment, he figured she never took him seriously.

"How are you dealing with it? Other than being hundreds of miles away? Is that working for you?"

"A little. I don't have to see him every day or risk the chance of running into him. I don't have to live in that house where he may have brought his mistress for their rendezvous. So it's helping. I need time to clear my mind and that's what I'm getting here."

"I see." Shane decided not to take the conversation any further. He smiled at her and changed the subject to reminiscing about old times. Although he didn't mention it, in the back of her mind, she replayed the events of the night he told her he loved her. She was home visiting her parents and he was home too. She had to study and he had a presentation that he had to give at the police academy, so they both thought it was a good idea to study together and hang out afterward.

Looking back on it, she wasn't sure why she ever agreed to such an arrangement, because they were so close that all they ever did when they were together was talk and play around. That night wasn't any different. She studied for maybe an hour tops. Somehow they ended up wrestling after she asked him to show her some of the moves taught to the new recruits at the police academy. Once she gave up and he pinned her to the floor, the mood suddenly changed. He leaned in to brush her lips with a kiss. It wasn't just any old kiss either. It wasn't a kiss that best friends share. There was emotion and passion behind that kiss. It must have lasted all of ten seconds, and if she closed her eyes and thought of it, she could still feel his lips against hers. She mindlessly rubbed her lips at the thought, totally missing everything that Shane had just said.

"Did you hear me?" Shane asked. He didn't miss the gesture and could only hope that she was thinking about the kiss they shared years ago. He wondered if she remembered that he told her he loved her.

"Of course I did!" She lied as she burst into laughter. "Say it again."

"You're so silly. How are your parents?"

"They're good. I haven't gone by their house yet. . .they don't know I'm here."

"Are you serious?"

Chloe nodded and reminded him that she'd only been in town a few days. She didn't want to hear about how her parents stuck it out and how they'd been married a hundred years. None of that stuff was helpful to her right now. She was dealing with a lot of hurt. Now if someone could tell her how to love and trust Rico again, that would be more helpful. She wasn't interested in anything else.

"Sista Chloe! Have you gone to the Lord about this thang?" Shane impersonated their pastor, which made Chloe burst into laughter again. Everyone kept telling her that, and she really was trying. But right now, it wasn't working for her.

"Your impersonation of him is dead on! I'm sure he would say that. Seriously though, I have prayed about it and sometimes I have no words. I know that God hates divorce, but I just don't see any other way through this. We've been trying to work on our marriage for a while now, and it's just not working. It was hard enough to keep things together with my work schedule and then he stepped out on me. The cheating definitely set us back. And it's hard for me to trust him again," Chloe said and shrugged her shoulders before taking a sip of water.

Shane knew that it was wrong for him to be excited at the thought of her marriage falling apart, but he couldn't help himself. He successfully masked his personal approval of her failing nuptials. He steered clear of giving her advice as to not sway her in any way, but promised to pray that God would lead her to make the best decision. He selfishly wanted that decision to be *end the marriage,* because he would be right there to help her pick up the pieces and help mend her broken heart.

CHAPTER 9

Kelly wanted to fuss at Chloe for seeing Shane. It seemed as if everyone was aware of Shane's feelings for Chloe, except Chloe—unless she knew and just chose to ignore them. Either way, Kelly didn't think it was a good idea for her to be going on dates with him. She didn't care that they grew up together; she was of the opinion that Chloe's thoughts should be centered on what she was going to do about her marriage.

"Sooo . . . how was lunch with Shane yesterday?" Kelly probed since it seemed as if Chloe was never going to talk about it. In Kelly's mind, it was a big deal.

Chloe shrugged off the obvious disapproval in Kelly's voice. Shane was her childhood friend; they decided years ago not to pursue a romantic relationship because their friendship was more important, although a small part of her always wondered what things could have been like between the two of them.

"It was good seeing him again. I can't remember the last time we sat down and had a bite to eat together. It was almost like old times. I guess I should count myself favored that it was Shane who pulled me over and not another cop," Chloe said and smiled, trying to ease her sister's worries.

"Umm hmm," Kelly said as she sipped her mug of chai tea and eyed her sister suspiciously.

"What? It's just Shane . . . you're acting like I've run off with him. Trust me. We're only friends."

"Okay, then. I guess it's settled." Kelly avoided the urge to lecture her big sister. She pondered Chloe's words and watched her demeanor. Her sister was surely acting like she'd been on a date. Just a few days ago, her eyes were dead, and now she was walking around looking like she'd won the lottery. Kelly tried to put herself in Chloe's shoes. What would she do if she were Chloe? She made it her personal mission to make sure things didn't go too far and to remind Chloe why she was in town—to think and not to start some hot summer romance. If Chloe weren't married, Kelly would be rooting for Shane since he was such a great guy, but that wasn't the case.

"So," Kelly asked, "seeing as though Rico's sisters have been a thorn in your side since the wedding, what do they have to say about this temporary split?"

"Ah, girl." Chloe rolled her eyes, "I don't know, but knowing them, they're probably thrilled. That's one thing I for sure won't miss if we call it quits. They really irked my nerves," Chloe responded, grimacing at the thought of them.

"I know. Sorry you've had to deal with that throughout your marriage. Marriage can be tough without your in-laws butting in and making things worse."

Chloe recalled the time she first met Rico's three older sisters. They grilled her about her background, her family, her education and her intentions toward their brother. They made it perfectly clear that they loved their brother, but Chloe thought that they often went too far in the way they chose to show that love.

As co-pastor, Rico's mother took over as pastor of their church when their father passed away. Ever since then, they, especially the oldest sister, felt like it was their duty to look out for their mother and one another. Diane, the oldest sister, often called or texted Chloe rude and disrespectful messages, often using profanity for no reason or starting an argument just because she was in the mood for a fight. Chloe would never forget the Thanksgiving that she and Rico were planning to go see her family in Nashville and Diane put up a fight because they were planning a surprise dinner for their mom and they thought Rico should be there—though Rico knew nothing about the dinner until the last minute. Chloe was sure that Diane planned it to spite her when she found out that she and Rico were planning to travel for the holiday. Nevertheless, Rico felt bad about not being there, so Chloe ended up travelling alone while he went to the surprise dinner.

Chloe shook off the funk that she was slowly getting into at the thought of her in-laws.

"When I met Rico's family, I knew that there would probably be a problem with his sisters, but never did I think they'd treat me like some sort of outcast. It's like they do things intentionally to upset me. Remember that time Diane planned that cruise for the family reunion when she found out I had planned a cruise for Rico's thirtieth birthday? She did that so that no one would participate in the event I organized. You remember, don't you? You and your husband were the only ones who came with us. Or that time I had to put them out of my house because of her blatant disrespect?" Chloe recalled what happened that day.

Chloe's ears perked up at the sound of her name being dragged through the mud. She had been sitting at the kitchen table thumbing through the latest issue of O magazine while Rico stood at the stove cooking breakfast. He was much better at cooking grits and flipping pancakes than she was, so making breakfast was his one kitchen duty whenever they got a chance to sit down and eat together. Because of her hectic work schedule at the hospital, that was hardly ever.

"Can you believe that?" Diane huffed in her normal rude tone, especially when referring to Chloe. Her voice was low, but loud enough to make it known to Chloe that the conversation was about her.

The other two sisters mumbled something but Chloe couldn't make out what it was. Again, Diane repeated her question. Chloe glanced toward Rico and frowned.

"Who is she talking about? What is she talking about?" Chloe asked Rico, her voice raising an octave. She was becoming frustrated at the thought that Diane had the nerve to be talking about her while sitting in her house. Rico hunched his shoulders, ignoring the chatter coming from the living room, and continued flipping pancakes. He never stood up for her, and it didn't appear that he was about to start that day. Chloe pushed away from the table and walked over to the living room entryway, pausing with her arms folded.

"Can you believe she has the nerve to sit there reading a magazine while Rico is standing over a hot stove cooking? What's wrong with this picture? No wonder he cheated," Diane grumbled.

Nearly burning his hand, Rico immediately switched the burners off and hustled toward the living room. He knew his sister didn't care for his wife, but he couldn't believe she would go that far.

At the sound of Rico's footsteps approaching from behind, Chloe flung one hand in the air, daring him to take another step.

"Now you wait one minute," Chloe said to them. "I could care less what your feelings are about me, but you will not disrespect me in my own house. Get your crap together and leave. I'll call you an Uber and you can have the driver take you wherever you need to go, as long as it's away from here!" Chloe spat. She was in no mood to go into battle with Diane. She usually kept her silence while Diane mumbled her displeasure under her breath, but she was not going to take it in her own home.

The sisters all gasped, eyes wide, shaking their heads, not believing that Chloe was threatening to put them out.

"Ricky, you're just gonna stand there?" Diane questioned, surprised that Rico wasn't taking up for them or putting Chloe in her place. After all, it was his house too.

"Husband you live with me. If you feel the need to speak up now, you can get your things too. We will see y'all at the wedding tomorrow, but don't think you'll spend another moment in my house talking about me like I'm not here. Get your rags and get the hell out!"

Chloe pulled her cell phone out of her back pocket, opened the Uber app and did as she promised. She glanced toward Rico, her eyes burning with disgust and anger, daring him to protest.

Although they were working on their marriage, that would have been all the reason she needed to put the nail in the coffin.

Chloe kept her post at the entryway between the living room and the kitchen, waiting for the Uber to arrive. For the next fifteen minutes, no one said a word. The sisters each waited on the couch with incredulous looks on their faces, suitcases parked in front of them, waiting for their ride. Diane shot Chloe a few evil glances, but Chloe ignored them. It took everything within her not to unleash the years of biting her tongue and the desire to strangle her neck.

The breakfast that Rico had been making sat on the stove growing cold. No one had the stomach to eat. And as far as Chloe was concerned, they weren't welcome to be in her home anymore, let alone eat there. The other sisters didn't say much to tick Chloe off, but they agreed with Diane. If they were to all sit down at the table, she couldn't guarantee that she wouldn't use a piece of silverware in a manner that it wasn't designed for; she was at her wits' end with all of their mess. What made matters worse is that Rico never stepped in to put his sisters in their place.

Her phone rang, alerting her that the Uber driver was outside. To keep from saying something that would make the situation even worse, Chloe remained silent with one raised eyebrow and tilted her head toward the door. Diane angrily snatched the handle on her suitcase, with her sisters following closely behind.

With an exasperated breath, Rico ran after them. He couldn't leave things that way. The least he could do was take them to their destination. He paid the driver for his time and directed his sisters to get into his car so that he could take them to a hotel.

Kelly burst into laughter at the thought of Chloe putting anyone out of her house. Chloe giggled a little at the incident now that it was far behind them.

"Diane is so evil. But at least I know her level of mischief. The others barely even acknowledge my existence."

"I'm sorry sis." Kelly placed her mug on the kitchen table and walked around to her sister to embrace her. Chloe continued to lean against the refrigerator after accepting her sister's hug. Just the thought of Rico's sisters was enough to rush the ending of her marriage, but she knew she couldn't allow them to be the reason that she ended it for good if that was her decision.

"Yeah, me too. It's a shame that things have to be this way between us."

"What have you done to try to mend, well I guess the proper word would be 'forge,' a relationship with those sisters of his?"

Chloe shrugged. She may not have tried hard enough to make things work with Diane and her siblings, but they were the ones who should have been trying to welcome her into the family, not push her away.

"I always invite them over for holiday dinners, whenever I'm off work and get a chance to do that. They always say they're coming but they never show up. The real problem is that Rico doesn't see a problem with how they treat me, though most of it is done slyly."

"What does he say or do exactly?"

"He just brushes it off saying things like, 'That's just how they are.' But whether that's true or not, that does not excuse their behavior, and I refuse to allow them to treat me any kind of way. So I usually stay behind and work when he goes to Alabama to visit them."

Chloe's venting was interrupted by her phone. The ringer volume decreased when she picked up the phone to check the caller. *Speak of the devil,* she thought. Without answering it or acknowledging the caller, she placed the phone back on the table.

"You're not gonna answer? Who was that?"

"Diane. I guess her brother must have finally given them the news."

Kelly shook her head in disapproval but didn't comment. A missed opportunity. She wanted Chloe to answer the phone so that she could tell Diane to kick rocks and mind her own business, something she knew that Chloe would probably bite her tongue and not say, trying to be respectful. Diane had some nerve calling and stirring the pot, considering her brother was the one who messed up. To help Chloe clear her mind for a while, Kelly suggested they go out for a little retail therapy before the kids came home from school. When Chloe agreed and walked away to change clothes, Kelly picked up Chloe's phone. It was locked and Kelly didn't know her passcode. She wasn't sure what she would have done had it not been locked. Call Rico? Call Diane? Surely Chloe would kill her twice over because she likely would have made the situation worse. She was torn between giving Rico a piece of her mind and trying to figure out a way to help them through it. Though the thought of her sister getting a divorce broke her heart, she wanted her to be at peace.

She put the phone down and trotted up the stairs, thinking of a way to help her sister without imposing too much. All she wanted was to see her sister happy, and if Rico didn't get his act together, that happiness was going to be with Shane, regardless of how much Chloe tried to convince herself otherwise.

CHAPTER 10

"She left you? Well you know she wasn't good enough for you anyway! We all knew that. It's about time you know it, too!" Diane went on and on with the help of her sisters singing *Amen* to her every word. This was just the ammunition Diane needed to support her belief that Chloe was no good for Rico or their family.

Rico was starting to regret his impromptu visit to Alabama. What had he gotten himself into? For a moment, he thought it would be comforting to be around family instead of lying in bed every night in that empty house with only the sound of dogs howling and crickets chirping to keep him company. He planned to take the advice of both Pastor Lewis and his friend Michael, but he made the decision, which he was now coming to regret, first to come home to be with his family.

Rico shook his head in disbelief at Diane. He had never understood why she hated his wife so much. He had always defended her to Chloe, but he was beginning to see that Diane truly held a grudge against Chloe and he had no idea why. Before he knew it, she'd whipped her phone out and begun to call Chloe to chew her out. Luckily for all of them, Chloe didn't answer. He didn't want her to think that he went crying to his family or that he needed his sisters or anyone else to fight his battles. Besides, he needed someone in his corner who would convince her to come back to him and not stay away. Neither Diane nor his other sisters would be able to assist him in the way that he desperately needed.

Rico's mom might have some answers. However, she was a pastor too, so he pretty much knew what type of advice she would give. He needed something practical and no one was giving him that. Pray. Sure, he'd do that. But what else? What did God need him to do to get his wife to come home ASAP?

"Actually," Rico said aloud, "Chloe was the best thing that ever happened to me. I was the one who messed up, Diane, not her. And I would appreciate it if you would show her some respect. You don't have to like her but you will respect her. She is my wife," Rico retorted. He tried his best not to allow his true feelings to show. He was pissed at Diane for the way she was acting, with no regards to his feelings or his desire to keep his marriage. If he'd allow his emotions to take over, it would be World War III—and he didn't have time for that right now. He didn't want to waste energy arguing with her.

"You are my brother and I love your big-head self," she admitted, giving him a kiss on the forehead before walking back over to the stove to check on her dinner rolls. "But I don't trust her and I never have. I won't talk about her anymore," she said before mumbling, "at least not in front of you." And she meant it. She hadn't ever cared for Chloe, but the moment Chloe put them out of her house, that was the end for Diane. She'd never felt so humiliated nor did she ever expect that from Chloe, especially since she'd always been so meek before.

The other sisters giggled at Diane's antics while they sat around the small kitchen table in their mother's home, as they often did. Her family was used to her outspoken and often rude behavior, but none of them ever said anything to correct her. It was entertainment for them. That is probably what bothered Diane the most about Chloe. Chloe putting them out of her house was an attempt to set her straight, and she would never get over that. That move was a kick to her ego.

"I don't think you heard anything I just said, girl! I cheated on her, so she has every right to be upset with me and do whatever she is doing right about now," Rico yelled in frustration. He rested his head in his palms, rubbing his temples, trying to reduce the headache that was quickly starting to develop. He was beginning to think that his sister would never change. It was one thing that she was often rude with her siblings when she wasn't getting her way, but it was another thing that she continued to treat his wife and marriage with such disrespect.

"Even though I don't like her, I have to tell you that you're wrong for cheating on her. Probably could have avoided all of this if you had taken my advice and not married her stuck-up tail in the first place! Why were you cheating? How did you get caught?" Diane chastised and probed all at once.

"It just happened," was all Rico could say. There was no explaining things to Diane, especially since he knew she would just gossip about him behind his back and probably in his face too.

"Umm hmm," Diane didn't buy his response for one second. She sized him up, trying to figure out possible reasons why he would have cheated.

"So, was she working too much? Not giving you any? C'mon, you have to give me something here! Men don't just cheat; they have to have a reason," she pushed. In her experience, the many times she was the cheater or the one being cheated on, there was always a reason. Usually something small that eventually festered, but cheating never just happened.

"Diane!" Sandra, the second oldest sister, shrieked. "Can't you see he isn't going to tell you?"

Diane rolled her eyes and waved Sandra off. She had to get to the bottom of this. She turned back to Rico, beckoning him with her eyebrows to answer her questions. She needed a reason to blame Chloe anyway, so that she could feel justified for not liking her in the first place. When she saw that Rico wasn't opening up, she asked him to at least tell her how Chloe found out about his mistress.

"My phone. Chloe answered when she called to tell me about the baby." Rico's answer caused the room full of sisters to fall silent. They hadn't realized just how serious his relationship with his mistress had been. He knew that would shut them up. He even surprised himself by revealing that much information to them. But at least they were women and could help him understand things from a woman's point of view. Up until now, he'd only really had the advice of Michael and Pastor Lewis.

"Well dang! A baby, Rico? How could you have been so stupid! No wonder she left your butt! I don't know too many women who will stick around with you after that. That's a lot to get over," Sandra chimed in again. Sandra was usually the more reasonable sibling, so Rico had no problem listening to her.

"So where is the baby now?" Diane wanted to know. "We have a niece or nephew and you never told us? Does Momma know?"

"There is no baby; she lost it," Rico commented. He now remained silent, forefinger and thumb rustling with the hairs on his chin as he thought of Raegan and the baby. He wondered what would have happened if he didn't sign over his parental rights. Would the baby have survived? He figured he wouldn't even tell his sisters about him giving up his rights; they would surely flip out. There was no use getting into all of that now since there was no baby to even fight over. He was sure Diane would be trying to fight to have the baby in their lives if for no other reason than to spite Chloe.

The room fell silent again. Just as quickly as they all became excited about a baby, their hearts broke for the loss of it. Just when Rico thought that the questions had ceased, Diane turned the oven and the burners off and sat in the empty chair next to him.

"I promise this is my last question for today about all of this, and I will leave it alone. How did Chloe take the news of the baby?" She despised her so much that she really only wanted to know so that she could rejoice in Chloe's pain. She knew it was wrong, but in some twisted way, it gave her a little joy knowing that she had gotten a kick in the butt from the heavens.

Rico shook his head at her. The look in her eyes gave her away. He knew that she didn't sympathize for his wife but only wanted to know for her own perverse reasons. He reckoned he may as well tell the story now or else he would have to do it again later. That way, they could tell his mother so that he wouldn't have to. He couldn't bear the disappointment that he knew would be reflected in her eyes.

"She was pretty pissed, especially since that's a stage in our relationship that we hadn't gotten around to. And for it to happen with someone else—" Rico blew an audibly frustrated breath before continuing. "I never meant for her to get pregnant and I wish I hadn't hurt Chloe in that way. I really regret it and I wish there was something I could do to take it all back, but I can't." Rico punched his hand to emphasize his point. The more he thought about the whole ordeal, the angrier he became with himself.

"Nah, you can't," Diane said thoughtfully. She seemed satisfied enough with his answer as her wheels turned with all the ways she could throw this in Chloe's face out of spite, but kept her promise to not ask another question about his cheating or use it as fuel in her arsenal, at least for the time being.

"Where is Momma?" Rico asked. Quite a few hours had passed and she hadn't returned home yet. He remembered that he told Raegan that it was only him and his mom. Some days he wished that were true because his sisters could really be a handful; he was certain they would hate Raegan just as much, or even more than, they hated Chloe. They seemed to despise her because she was college-educated and from a well-rounded family. Chloe and Raegan were pretty much the same in that department. He chuckled to himself. Although Raegan hated him for lying to her, she would be grateful to know that she dodged a bullet when it came to the family she knew nothing about.

"Where she always is . . . at that church," Sandra answered, her voice a little snappy. Ever since their mom took over as pastor, each of them felt neglected in some way. They tried not to complain because they knew she was doing the best she could, trying to carry on their father's legacy. Their mom had always hoped that Rico would take over the church, but that was the furthest thing from Rico's mind. He couldn't live the life he wanted to live being a pastor. But maybe he wouldn't be in the mess he was in right now if he were living his life like he was supposed to be living it.

"All right, I'm going to take a walk and then rest up. Somebody come get me when she comes home. Well, I take that back—I think I'll go by the church and surprise her," Rico said, changing his mind. Instead of taking the cowardly way out, he decided that he should be the one to tell his mother about his crumbling marriage to Chloe, though he didn't plan to tell her about the baby; that would probably tear her apart just as much as it did Chloe. He knew that Diane would turn it all around on Chloe to make it seem as if it were all her fault, if she talked to their mother first. He had done the dirt and he would own up to it.

CHAPTER 11

Shane knew that lawfully, Chloe was still married to Rico, but that fact didn't negate the feelings that his heart held captive for her. He was glad that she agreed to meet with him again, as friends. His intentions were entirely pure, or at least that is what he told himself. But given the right opportunity, he wouldn't hesitate to do whatever it would take to make Chloe his forever.

Country Music Hall of Fame and Museum. He wasn't sure if Chloe would enjoy it entirely, but it was one of the top things to do while in Nashville.

"As a kid I always dreamed of coming here," Chloe remarked as she stepped out of her car. Shane reached for her hand to help her out.

"No way. Are you making fun of me?" Shane felt a sense of relief that he'd made the right choice in bringing her there. That was a sign that they would likely have a good time. Country music wasn't his favorite but he'd listen to it every now and again. Besides, there was no way around it; he heard it in just about every restaurant or store he visited.

"Nope, scouts honor," she said and held two fingers in the air. She enjoyed country music secretly because her mother blasted it as loud as possible on her stereo when she was a child, and she would never admit liking it to her mother. She knew and loved practically every Reba McEntire and Trisha Yearwood song.

"So you're telling me you actually enjoy country music?" Shane asked, still a tad bit skeptical.

"A little." She shrugged as she walked past him. Inside, Chloe noted there was an exhibit dedicated to her favorite country star, Steven Mark Sumpter, which was only planned to be in the museum for one more month. She counted herself lucky. She had to see it first. He'd been to Houston many times to play during the Houston rodeo, but Rico would never go with her and none of her friends liked country music. She had to settle to listening to his music on her iPod since she didn't want to attend the show alone. But now, she had the opportunity to see several Steven Mark Sumpter artifacts firsthand.

Noting directions, she aggressively pulled Shane in the direction so that she could admire the exhibit: Country is Who I Am. To say she was a huge fan was a complete understatement.

She could spot anything of his from a mile away, and when she quickly found the location of the exhibit, Shane stood by, chest puffed up, pleased with himself for choosing the museum. The only people he'd known to love country music were his co-workers' wives.

"Want to tell me about some of this stuff?" he asked, breaking her fixation on the Steven Mark Sumpter pieces.

Chloe pointed out the guitar he played on the CMA Awards when he first sang the song he wrote after the 9/11 terrorist attacks. The very first toy guitar he owned as a toddler was on display. They also saw his first tricycle, bike, and scooter, all things that she read about being in the museum. She described the history of the belt buckles—straight from the Houston rodeo! Shane was amazed at her knowledge of all things Steven Mark Sumpter; he had no idea that she would be such a fan of his and an avid listener of country music. And to think he thought he knew just about everything about her.

Chloe snapped a few pictures of the exhibit with her cell phone and even a couple of selfies of her and Shane in front of the exhibit so that she could be forever reminded of the day. It wasn't every day that she would get a chance to walk into the Country Music Hall of Fame and Museum.

Even though Shane had known Chloe most of his life, he felt like he was closer to her than before because she opened up a side of herself that she hadn't allowed anyone to see for fear that they wouldn't understand or share her enthusiasm for all things country.

Their last stop in the museum before leaving was the Hall of Fame Rotunda. Chloe marveled at pictures of all of her favorite musicians and her mom's favorites, hanging on the wall; she even took selfies beside some of them, including Shane in some of them as well. Shane held the door for her as they walked out of the museum. Chloe was on cloud nine from the excitement of doing something she'd wanted to do since she was about fifteen. Her mom had gone a few times, but as a rebellious teenager, she wouldn't have been caught dead inside that establishment with her mother. Now she saw everything that she had missed out on. Of course, it was much better now than it would have been back then.

"Thanks, Shane!" Chloe squealed and threw her arms around his neck. That certainly helped to keep her mind off her troubles with Rico. In fact, she hadn't thought about him much over the past few days. Part of her was trying to push him as far away from her mind as possible, but the other part knew that she had to make a decision.

"Anything for you! I'm just glad that I could brighten your day. Say, do you have anything planned for July 4th?" Shane asked timidly. He was praying she would say no.

"No, what's going on? It's been so long since I've spent so much time here. What do you guys do around here to celebrate?"

"How about you let me show you? We can meet on the riverfront," Shane suggested casually.

"Sounds like a plan to me," Chloe agreed. *What am I doing? Is this a date?* Chloe questioned herself. She wondered if she should be carrying on like this with Shane. She was certain both he and her sister would start getting the wrong idea if she kept spending time with him. The problem was that she liked hanging out with him. It almost felt like old times. He had once been a very good friend of hers, and as far as she was concerned, they were merely catching up.

Shane hugged her once more. Before she could pull away and climb into her car, Shane did what he wanted to do ever since he pulled her over for speeding a couple of weeks ago. His lips touched hers. He immediately wanted to pull back and apologize for fear of her thinking that he was moving too fast, crossing the line, or trying to sway her mind with everything going on with her husband. But before he could complete his thought, he realized that she was kissing him back, forgetting about the cars passing by and everything else that mattered in the world. In his mind, they became the twenty-somethings who got swept up in the moment way back when. But they were no longer in their twenties and their situation was totally different and way more complicated. *Now what?*

CHAPTER 12

"What would your father say about this, Ricky?" his mother spewed, not looking him in the eye, calling him by his childhood name. He expected a little more compassion from her, but he should have known better. She was always more concerned about what the church would think than the feelings of her children, at least so he thought. Whether it was getting in trouble in school or on the streets, Rico felt like his mother always handled it from the standpoint of protecting her image at church and not necessarily showing him and his sisters the love and attention they deserved.

Rico plopped down in the chair in her office across from her desk; the only answer to her question was the sound of the clock ticking and the soft chatter down the hallway. He didn't answer her question because she and he both knew that his father would be disappointed and he hated that she chose to remind him of that. Besides, he knew he messed up; he really just wanted her to tell him how to fix it. She had always been so good at fixing public image so that it wouldn't reflect badly on the family; he was hoping that this wouldn't be any different.

"Ricky! Look at me. What on God's green earth were you thinking? Have you been praying and studying God's Word like I taught you?" Her eyes narrowed as she studied his face. God's Word promised that if you taught your children God's ways when they were young, they wouldn't depart from it when they were older. Perhaps Rico hadn't reached the *old* that the Scripture mentioned, because he certainly wasn't acting like she taught him anything.

Rico's face was covered with disappointment and hurt as he fixed his eyes on the mole in the center of his mother's forehead that she tried to hide with makeup. He didn't feel strong enough to look her in the eyes in that moment. No, he hadn't been praying or studying, at least not until recently. Before returning to his home church in Houston, the last time he had set foot in a church was when he surprised Raegan. *Sweet, beautiful Raegan.* Everything he did to pursue her started playing in his mind, but he quickly caught himself. He didn't need to think about her. His infatuation with her was what got him into the mess he was in now.

"Momma, I don't have any answers; I'm here looking for them," he said, admitting defeat.

Regina watched her son carefully, noticing the way he looked dejected sitting across from her. He heart went out to him as a mother. She walked over to him and leaned over and held him for a moment, something her husband would have chided her for. The late Pastor Remington would have had a fit. He always thought that she was too soft on him, coddled him too much, and didn't give him enough breathing room to be a man. But she wanted Rico to be better than his father was, and the moment she gave him his space, he started messing up. She was proud of him when he settled down and married Chloe, but the man sitting in her office now was not the man she raised.

"I need you to help me get my wife back." Rico's voice cracked. The words escaped his mouth without thinking.

His mother backed away and leaned into the desk. Those words must have struck a chord with her, because he could have sworn he saw fire flashing through her eyes. She truly had no sympathy for him.

"Ricky, if you want your wife back, you're going to have to stop cheating, start praying and get into the good Lord's Word. That is where all of your answers are. There is not much I can do for you, Son," she answered, her voice lacking any sort of emotion. Gone was the gentle woman who, just seconds ago, wrapped her arms around him telling him that it would be fine and that she loved him.

Rico shook his head in exasperation. He did not come into her office for her to tell him that. Why was everyone telling him the same thing? He needed definite answers. How was simply praying and reading the Bible going to help him get Chloe back? He needed some action items.

Regina's eyes grew cold and narrow as she spoke, remembering her own battle with her former husband's infidelity.

"At least your father had the decency not to procreate with his whores . . . as far as I know. You see, I know how Chloe must be feeling—unappreciated, used, frustrated, disappointed, confused and just absolutely pissed. Torn between trying to find peace and save face in front of your church. Wanting to choke the life out of the man who vowed to love and cherish you forever!" Her voice elevated as the feelings she'd suppressed rose to the surface. She'd never really gotten over the pain she felt, and her husband dying before she could make peace with the situation left her unsettled.

Rico sat there stunned, wondering if any of his sisters knew about this. Now he understood why his mother gave him that look—his indiscretions brought back all of the feelings she had when his father treated her the same way that he treated Chloe. His eyes grew hot with anger at the thought of his father mistreating her.

"Hold on a minute, Ricky. Don't forget that you did the same thing. His sins aren't any greater than your sins," she reminded him, wagging her finger, after seeing the look of resentment plastered across his face.

"I'm sorry; I'm truly sorry. To you and to Chloe. I had no idea." This was one time that Rico wished his father was alive so that he could confront him about treating his mother that way. But like his mother said, who was he to judge? Didn't he also cheat on his wife? In Rico's mind, this was different because this was his mother.

"Had you known, would that have kept you from cheating on your wife? Would you have avoided temptation and channeled that energy into your marriage instead of adultery with another woman?" his mother challenged him.

Ouch. Every time he heard the word *adultery* it churned his ears. *Cheating* may have been sugarcoating it, but he liked the way that sounded much better. Adultery sounded a lot like doom.

He didn't know if he would have done things differently had he known about his father's carelessness. But he definitely regretted being the reason that Chloe had been hurting for so long. Even though they tried to work things out, their marriage was never the same after the day in the coffee shop when he signed over his parental rights to Raegan. If he were Chloe, he probably wouldn't take him back, but he still had to try.

"So where is she now?"

Rico shrugged his shoulders. She never told him where she was going, but he suspected she went to Nashville if she left town. He hadn't tried to contact her because he was quite sure she didn't want to speak with him based on the last time he saw her in their home. Besides, he didn't know what to say. "Take me back" and pleading with her didn't seem to be enough. She needed to know that he was different and things would be different between them. She needed to know that he loved her with everything within him and he would do everything in his power to show her that until the end of his life. She needed to know that he was serious and that he was all in—like he should have been in the first place. And for now, he just didn't have the right words to say.

"Pastor Remington," a man's voice said while knocking and opening the door at once. Rico thought the voice sounded familiar. He turned in his seat to see Papa David, Chloe's father, entering his mother's office. Life just couldn't get any worse for Rico. If he could, he would have disappeared that very second.

CHAPTER 13

Chloe thoughtlessly ran her forefinger along her lips as she drove back to Kelly's home. She could still feel the imprint of Shane's lips pressed against hers. *What was I thinking?* she mused, her mind on autopilot. *Get it together Chloe. He's just a friend and you are still married,* she thought. She had to admit that something felt right about it. She didn't know if it was because she'd known Shane forever or the fact that her marriage was practically over anyway.

When she walked through the door, she noticed that Kelly had been waiting on her. Kelly patted the cushion next to her on the sofa with one hand, while with the other she held the chai tea she had been sipping. It didn't matter to her that it was nearly one hundred degrees outside; nothing could keep her away from her favorite drink.

"Hey sis," Chloe sang, trying hard to mask the tinge of excitement that she felt. She knew that Kelly would automatically assume that it was because of Shane and no doubt remind her that she was still married to Rico. Kelly didn't hide the fact that she believed Chloe should not be spending so much time with Shane, given she was still married to Rico, no matter what state her marriage was in. She didn't want her to come to regret anything should the circumstances change.

"Umm hmm. Hey big sis. Come on over, let's talk," she said, smiling over her mug and muting the TV.

"Sure, what's up? Where's my tea? Don't act like you weren't waiting for me to come through that door."

Kelly carefully set her mug on the table and ran into the kitchen, quickly re-entering the living room with a mug for Chloe. "So, tell me. How long are you planning to stay here again?"

"Kicking me out so soon?" Chloe teased.

"Never that. I'm just curious to know what your plans are." That was Kelly's way of indirectly trying to figure out if Chloe had been considering her marriage to Rico and whether or not she had made a decision to stay or leave him for good.

Chloe shrugged her shoulders as she took a sip of tea. "Maybe I'll get a job at the hospital," she said to feel her sister out.

"Then what will you do about your job back in Houston?"

"I'm not really worried about that. All of that can be worked out. Besides, I don't know yet if I'm going back to Houston. I kind of miss things here in Nashville," Chloe answered and grinned over her mug before taking a sip.

"Things or Shane?" Kelly asked, her eyebrows shot in the air while her mug was raised halfway to her lips. She seemed a little defensive.

Chloe knew that was coming, she just didn't know when. The honest answer was *both*. She was enjoying spending time with Shane again, even though they were only friends. And that kiss today? What did that mean? Chloe placed her mug on the coffee table and folded her legs underneath herself to get comfortable.

"What does Shane have to do with any of this? You do remember that we all grew up together, right?"

"Umm hmm. Except that you're forgetting that Shane has *always* had a thing for you. You're clearly the only person who doesn't see that, unless you're trying to ignore it. I never left Nashville and Shane has never invited me out. So . . .do you have a thing for him, too?" Kelly decided to go ahead and ask. She was curious and there was no reason to beat around the bush anymore. She wanted answers.

"Are you asking as my sister and confidant or as the marriage counselor who wants to send me packing back to my cheating husband?"

Kelly mimicked Chloe and placed her mug on the coffee table as well, curling her feet beneath her. She rested her head against her fist, making herself comfortable. She wanted Chloe to trust her as her sister. Besides, she couldn't really help Chloe if she wasn't privy to all of the details.

"I don't know," Chloe finally admitted. "I guess I've always thought of him as the friend next door. Never really romantically. He's definitely become quite a looker and it doesn't hurt that he's a gentleman. I suppose if I weren't in the situation that I'm in, I would definitely give him a chance. But I wouldn't bring him into this mess of a life I have right now. I don't even know what I'm going to do about my marriage. He's a nice guy, so he deserves more than that."

"That's true but tell me you know that he is head over heels for you, right?"

"You think so?" Chloe questioned, doing a terrible job of trying to mask the grin that fought to spread across her face. She just wanted to hear Kelly confirm it. Shane practically sealed that question in her mind when he kissed her earlier that day. She presumed that she'd done the same for him when she returned the kiss.

"Yes!" Kelly answered, swinging the couch pillow at Chloe, as if to knock some sense into her. "Just don't lead him on. Whatever you're doing with him, remember to be honest about where you stand, okay? The poor guy is wearing his heart on his sleeve, so don't take things too far with him; and if you ever get caught up in the moment, remember that you're still married to Rico. In fact, don't do anything you wouldn't want Rico doing."

Chloe nodded as Kelly went on giving her advice. She didn't care about preserving Rico's feelings, so the whole conversation about not doing what she didn't want Rico to do didn't really matter. He should have thought of that before he started seeing Raegan and God only knows who else.

Chloe's phone had been incessantly vibrating, so she excused herself to check the messages.

Shane: *I had a great time today. Can't wait to do it again. I know your situation and I'm not trying to rush you into anything. I will call you later. Going into work for a couple of hours. Shane.*

Chloe: *It's cool. I had a great time too. Talk later.*

"That's him, isn't it?" Kelly called from across the room.

Chloe nodded with a smile that showed nearly all of her teeth.

"So do me one favor. Admit that you know he has a thing for you. If you didn't know before, I *know* that you know by now. Admit it!" Kelly could see that Chloe was in good spirits and she was genuinely happy for her; she just hoped that Chloe wasn't giving Shane false hope. Her decision to end or keep her marriage no longer affected only her and Rico, it now involved Shane whether Chloe wanted it to or not.

Chloe giggled, put her phone back into her purse and walked out of the room without admitting anything to Kelly. Not even a minute later, she could hear Kelly's footsteps behind her.

"Chloe, do Mom and Dad know that you're here?" Kelly asked while simultaneously texting.

"No. Not yet, why?" Chloe knew that she would likely hear lectures from their parents since they'd been married nearly forty years. She wasn't ready to face them yet. She'd made sure that she didn't go anywhere they were likely to see her.

"Because Mom just texted me. They're in Alabama for a church conference, at your mother-in-law's church."

Chloe's heart sank as she tried to swallow the knot in her throat. This was not part of her plan. She knew that she couldn't keep her problems from her parents for too long now. It would take a miracle for them not to find out about her walking out on her marriage. She didn't know what Rico's mother knew, but if Diane was aware of her marital problems, that was enough. She knew Diane well enough to know that she would smear her name in every which way that she could; and now her parents would hear all about her crumbling marriage from everyone but her.

CHAPTER 14

David Harrison was taken by surprise when he saw his son-in-law sitting across from Pastor Remington. When he last spoke to Chloe, she didn't mention anything about coming to Alabama for Pastor Remington's annual church conference.

Rico stood as Papa David entered the study and extended his hand to him. He shook Rico's hand firmly but slowly as if he was trying to figure out what was going on. He glanced from one to the other, but neither offered any explanation as to why Rico was in Alabama.

"I'm surprised to see you here. Chloe didn't mention that you two were coming to visit. Where is she?" Papa David asked, sensing something wasn't right.

"She didn't come with me this time," was all Rico could offer. He thought of lying, but he didn't know which lie to tell and he didn't really want to lie standing in church. Rico pulled his hand away and stuffed it inside his jean pocket as he tried to prepare for the next question.

"Why not? Did she have to work?"

Rico wished that was the case right about now. That had always been his excuse to do whatever he wanted to do before, but he couldn't blame this one on her. *I'm going to be a man about it,* he thought.

"Mom, may I use your office to talk with Papa David for a few moments alone?" His eyes pleaded with her. It wasn't as if he was afraid of Chloe's father, but he had never wanted to stand in front of him and tell him that he cheated on his daughter. Not to mention that she left him, he didn't really know where she was and their marriage was practically over.

Pastor Remington walked over and gave her son a quick kiss on the cheek, hugged Deacon Harrison and left to go find his wife. When Rico heard the door quietly close behind her, he motioned for Papa David to take a seat. There was no easy way to break the news to him, especially since it seemed that this would be the first time he was hearing of it. Papa David had never been one to come across as threatening, but that didn't calm Rico's nerves. Who knew what he might do to him after learning that Rico had broken his daughter's heart?

Rico took a seat next to him, leaned forward with his elbows on his knees and hands clasped, offering up a silent prayer to Heaven.

"Chloe didn't come with me because she's gone. I messed up, so she left me." For a moment, the only thing that could be heard in the room was the sound of the ceiling fan turning on a low setting. Papa David glared at Rico for a while. Rico didn't know what to expect next. He wasn't sure if Papa David was going to hoist him up against the wall by his collar, take a knee and pray for him or use that loud booming voice of his to take whatever ounce of manhood he had left in him.

As a leader in the church, Papa David had seen this sort of thing more times than he could count. Before making any judgments or coming to any conclusions without getting the facts, he simply questioned what happened.

"Why did she leave you?" Papa David asked in a voice so calm that he surprised himself. He wondered why this was the first time he was hearing of it. Why hadn't he and his wife heard from Chloe? How long had she dropped off the face of the earth?

"I had an affair," Rico answered. He didn't talk about the baby or try to make excuses saying that it didn't mean anything, because it meant something. He did have feelings for Raegan; he just couldn't do anything with them. Besides, that was over. He loved his wife and he wanted to work things out with her; they had to get past this.

"What in God's name were you thinking, son?" There came the loud, audacious voice that matched Papa David's stature. Rico could feel all of his six-foot five-inch, three hundred pound frame in that question. He was almost afraid to look at him after that, but he knew that Papa David would certainly lose all respect for him now if he acted like a wimp. He did the deed, so he had to own up to it.

Rico leaned back in the chair and rested his head on the back of it. Everyone kept asking him that, but he didn't have the answers. *Maybe I wasn't thinking, only feeling.*

"Sir, I'm sorry; I'm trying to fix this. I want my wife back. I'm even going to continue counseling when I get back to Houston," Rico tried to convince himself and his father-in-law.

"As the father of your lovely wife, I want to kill you. As God's servant, I'm here to tell you that you have a lot of work to do. This isn't going to be some overnight process. You'll likely be making up for this mistake for quite a while because you're going to have to gain her trust back. Are you up for that?" Papa David asked, flexing his fists over and over at his side to keep from reaching out and strangling Rico's neck. As much as he wanted to step in and inflict bodily harm on Rico, it wasn't his fight. He kept reminding himself of that fact as he watched Rico cautiously.

"Yes, sir . . . whatever it takes," Rico answered. He maintained eye contact because he didn't want to lose any respect that Deacon Harrison may have had left for him. He had to get his wife back now. He somehow felt like he had to make up for his indiscretions and for that of his father as well. He couldn't treat Chloe like his father treated his mother; he was better than that. He'd heard pastors talk about generational curses and he wondered if this was one of them. If so, he vowed that it would stop with him. If he ever had a son, he would be sure to teach him to treat his wife right—with love, respect and fidelity.

Deacon Harrison waited, watching his son-in-law wrestle inwardly, and finally said, "Good. If I ever have to have this conversation with you again, I'm not sure that the servant part of me would win. Got that?"

"Yes, sir."

"Good. Now let me go find my wife." Papa David stood to leave the study. He was reminded of the time that infidelity almost shattered his own marriage, but if God could work things out for him and his wife, He could do it for anyone. It took everything in him not to let Rico be on the receiving end of the anger he felt way back when. He'd gotten past it, but to know that his daughter was going through the same thing put his mind in a totally different place.

"I swear this keeps getting worse and worse," Rico said to himself after Papa David left the study. When the door shut, he dropped to his knees, bent over the chair, let out a long breath to relax his mind and prayed again, "Lord, please show me what to do. I'm so lost, God, and I know that You are the only One who can help me. Everyone keeps pointing me to You and honestly, I don't know what that means, but my heart is open to receive Your guidance. I am ready to do things Your way. Amen."

CHAPTER 15

"Momma has been calling my phone for the past hour! What is that about?" Chloe asked Kelly, dangling her phone in the air as she eyed her suspiciously. "Did you tell her?"

"What?" Kelly asked, clearly confused. "About Rico? I'm sitting here with you. Of course not."

Chloe was convinced her mom knew what was going on with her and Rico. There was no other reason she would be calling like that. First his sister Diane, and now her mother was calling. The fact that her mother was in Alabama with his family didn't give Chloe any comfort either.

"How about this? Answer the phone and see why she's calling," Kelly advised, as that seemed the only logical solution to Chloe's speculations.

"I don't want to hear the disappointment in her voice. She's Mother, I know she somehow knows what's going on," said Chloe. Besides, neither of them could truly understand her woes; they had faithful husbands.

"Well you don't want to know why she's calling, now do you?" Kelly responded, taking a moment to sip her tea, as if to give Chloe something to think about.

"Ugh!" Chloe rolled her eyes heavenward and silenced her ringer once more.

Chloe figured she could at least hold her parents off until they made it back to Nashville. She didn't really want to have a relationship discussion over the phone, if at all. An inkling of frustration came over her as her phone buzzed in her hand. She assumed it was her mother bugging her about not answering her cell phone, but Shane's name blinking alongside the notification icon washed that frown from her face.

Shane: *Thinking of you. Looking forward to the fireworks with you on the 4th. I'll call you this evening when my shift is over. Ttys*

Chloe: *I'm excited too. Ttyl*

"Momma say something funny?" Kelly interrupted her sister's moment.

"Nah, that wasn't her. I'll be sure to talk to her when she gets back though. Listen, I'm going to the hospital to talk about that open temp position. There's a nurse out on maternity leave so they are looking to temporarily fill her position. I'll be back later, sis. Love you." Chloe was out of the door before Kelly could respond.

Since Chloe would be out for a while, Kelly called their mom to find out what was going on. If Chloe wouldn't call her, she would. She was her sister's counselor, keeper and everything in between, so she needed to know about everything going on, including what was happening in Alabama with Rico and his family.

"Is your sister in Nashville?" Kelly's mom asked upon answering the phone. No "hello." No "how are you." Straight to business. The moment Cynthia Harrison heard what was going on, she had to get to the bottom of it. Rico in one state and her daughter in another. She knew her daughters were close, and if Chloe were to be anywhere, it would be with Kelly. Cynthia covered the mouthpiece to the cell phone and mouthed to her husband that she had one of the girls on the line.

"What do you mean?" Kelly responded, not giving a straightforward answer. She had promised Chloe that she wouldn't tell their parents that she was in town, but it was pretty clear that the cat was out of the bag now.

"Child, I birthed you! I know when you're trying to hide something from me. So where is she now? And don't you dare try to cover for her."

"The hospital."

"Oh no, what's wrong?" she dramatized, grasping her chest and holding her breath.

"She's fine, Momma . . . just looking into something. You know Chloe." Kelly pressed her lips together hoping that she hadn't revealed too much information. Her mother would have a fit if she knew that Chloe was looking for a job. Chloe was headstrong though, and there was nothing that either of them could say to stop her anyway.

"Whew! I thought I was going to have to catch the first flight back that way," she said and clutched her chest. Even though Chloe was a nurse, her mother's mind went straight to the worst when hearing she was at the hospital.

As Papa David recounted the details of his conversation to his wife, she paused and questioned Kelly about every detail. How long had Rico been cheating? How long had Chloe known? Was she planning to work on her marriage or divorce him? Did she know that divorce was not an option? Especially for the Harrison family. Kelly didn't have much information to give. She wanted

Chloe to tell her own story. She had a few choice words about Rico's behavior and didn't want to taint Chloe's story with her feelings. Although she believed that Chloe should take a little more time to make a decision about her marriage, there were a few things that she wanted to do to Rico herself. She didn't take too kindly to anyone messing with her sister, especially after he stood in front of God and their family vowing to love and cherish her, and only her, for the rest of his life.

"Momma, everything is going to be fine, I just know it, so please stop worrying. Tell Dad that he can stop worrying too," Kelly continued when she was greeted with silence. "But we know that this is going to take some time. Chloe is hurting right now, so she needs her space. Let's give her that. Trust me, I want to intervene just as much as you do, but we have to take baby steps. Okay?"

"I'm the momma. I can take care of this." She pretty much dismissed everything Kelly had just said. She had her mind made up on how she was going to handle it. Chloe just needed to hear from her.

"Gotta go Momma. I love you," Kelly said and blew a kiss through the phone.

"Love you too. Bye Kel."

Kelly had to go before she said too much and before her mom started to rant about how she knew what was best. She would be giving her whole "I'm the Momma" speech. There was so much more that her momma didn't know. There was Shane—handsome, eligible, head-over-heels-for-Chloe Shane. *Chloe likes him. He likes her. That complicates things. If Chloe stays and continues to see him, that will only make matters worse and pull her further and further away from Rico*—exactly where she wanted to be at the moment.

"So was she there?" Papa David asked after his wife ended the call.

"She's there all right, and you know what that means?"

Papa David shook his head, encouraging her to tell him what it meant. Never mind they'd been married forever, he still couldn't read her mind, although she frequently acted as if he could.

"The boy next door," she stated matter-of-factly, tapping her cell phone on her chin before dropping it into her shoulder bag. Cynthia knew that Shane was in love with her daughter from the very beginning. Even as teenagers, his eyes gave him away. She was surprised that he and Chloe never dated, but this time around, she feared that Shane wouldn't let her go. "What do you mean 'the boy next door'?" Papa David asked, still confused.

"Shane," she answered as if he should know who she was talking about. Although he didn't live next door to them anymore, his parents were still there, and in her mind, he should have understood. It wasn't as if there was anyone else who had lived next door and had eyes for their daughter. Their house was on the corner so they didn't have any other neighbors.

"What does Shane have to do with any of this?" He was clueless, considering he never really paid much attention to the two of them that way. Shane was like a son to him and Chloe never seemed to treat him like anything other than a brother, so Shane was the one guy he trusted around her. And although his wife had mentioned her suspicions before, he always thought it to be a figment of her imagination.

"Trust me. He will have everything to do with it from now on," she said thoughtfully. It was about time that Chloe learned the truth about her parents' marriage so that she could see that it was possible to get past infidelity and have a thriving, loving marriage again.

∞

Rico felt that the walls were about to suffocate him when he glanced up from his mother's chair to see his in-laws and mother entering the study. He knew the proper thing to do was to get up and give his mother her chair and greet his in-laws, but his bottom was glued to the seat. His feet felt like they were trapped in drying cement. He wasn't sure if they were about to gang up on him about his indiscretions or pour anointing oil on him and lay hands on him.

As a mother, Cynthia Harrison was on fire. She was not nearly as calm as Papa David had been when he spoke to him earlier that day. Her heart was hurting. For a moment, it felt like she was the one who had been cheated on. She could only imagine how her daughter must be feeling since she put their father through the same thing, and now her daughter was the one on the receiving end of the pain. Maybe it was her punishment for cheating so long ago; that is what hurt the most. She was the person in Rico's shoes over thirty-five years ago, so she was compelled to show mercy. But she recalled the heartache that she caused her husband and how she almost destroyed her family. Her prayer for Chloe when she got married was that she would never have to experience that kind of pain. And now here she was face to face with the person who caused that same type of pain to her daughter.

"I'm disappointed in you, Ricky," Cynthia Harrison finally spoke. "You do everything in your power to make things right with Chloe. And once you have done everything in your power, you work through the power of God." She was speaking from experience. She knew that the guilt would likely eat him up for the rest of his life and he would spend that long trying to make up for what he'd done—at least that was true for her. She looked at him and continued, "Do not give up on her. It's going to take a lot of time and it's not going to be easy, but you do whatever it takes . . . that is, if you want to save your marriage."

"I do. But I don't know what to do," Rico admitted with his head handing low. He spoke slowly through clenched teeth. It was becoming frustrating for everyone to keep telling him to make things right but not telling him how to do that.

He continued, "I've been trying for about a year now. The trust is gone. I don't know how to get it back. I don't even think she wants me back." Neither of them had reached out to their family for advice, so to find out that this had been going on for a year stunned everyone in the room.

"Get yourself right with the Lord first. That's what you do. And I don't mean just go to church on Sundays. I mean, really seek Him. Your prayer time needs to become your food. You're going to have to be all in," Cynthia Harrison said, her voice racked with emotion, both from remembering the pain she'd caused and thinking about the pain that her daughter must be going through.

Regina Remington walked around to where he sat and placed her hand on his shoulder. "She's right, Son. This isn't going to be a 'baby I'm sorry, please come home' type of thing. You're going to have to work harder than you did to win her the first time." Regina thought of the many chances she gave as she forgave her husband for his indiscretions. It was never easy and truth be told, part of her still held on to some of it.

"Yes ma'am. I've started counseling sessions with my pastor and I plan to keep going when I get back to Houston."

"Is Chloe going to be a part of these sessions?" His mother leaned back and looked at him. Everyone in the room had raised eyebrows.

"It's just me. But once I can get myself together, I hope to convince her to join with me." Rico's voice cracked a little, as he thought about Chloe's parting words to him, *I don't love you.* Chloe made it perfectly clear that she didn't want any part of him, but if she could see that he was a changed man and that he was truly trying, then maybe she'd change her mind. He just hoped that divorce papers weren't waiting on him when he returned to Houston.

That would be an even bigger problem.

CHAPTER 16

The fourth of July couldn't come fast enough. Shane had been anticipating this day for the past few weeks. They'd been out for coffee on two occasions and ice cream on another, but none of those outings were long enough for him. He couldn't wait to get another chance to see behind the soul of those dark brown eyes. A chance to show her what could be waiting on the other side for her if she chose to end her marriage to Rico. He would never treat her the way Rico did, and he needed her to see that, should she ever decide that Rico was no longer a suitable mate.

Instead of meeting her at the Riverwalk as originally planned, he picked her up from her sister's home. She only agreed to the change of plans once she knew that her sister would not be around to give her heartache about spending time with Shane. Kelly had already decided that Chloe shouldn't be spending any time with Shane, and instead should be spending that time thinking about the direction of her marriage. But Chloe couldn't agree less. Why would she spend time sulking about her failing marriage when she could be surrounding herself with positive things and people, stuff that made her smile and forget about her troubles?

Shane leaned against the passenger side of his Dodge Ram truck, careful to look as smooth as possible, although he knew that she would find the move quite entertaining. Since they grew up together, it seemed that he had to exaggerate his intentions to show her that he was seriously interested—he hoped that kiss was clear enough. He no longer wanted to be seen as only the guy next door. He wanted her to see him as the guy who had always been head over heels in love with her, would do anything for her, and wanted the best for her, even when she didn't think it was him.

When Shane saw the front door fling open, he slyly peeked at his reflection in the side view mirror to make sure that his eyes, nose and teeth were clean. He couldn't look smooth if foreign objects were on his face.

"You look like a man ready to have a good time," Chloe complimented his choice of clothes. Shane wore a burnt orange polo shirt coupled with khaki cargo shorts and a pair of loafers. His mustache was neatly shaven and his haircut looked as if he was straight out of the barber's chair. His cologne was a soft masculine scent, something that she hadn't smelled before, but suited him quite well.

"Spoken by a woman who only has to wake up to show the world her beauty," Shane returned the compliment. "Your carriage awaits," Shane said and bowed before he opened the door. He took care to clean his truck earlier that day in preparation for this moment. He wanted everything to be perfect. At least as perfect as it could be, since they were only going to watch the firework show. Perfect could just as well be not getting set on fire by a random spark.

Chloe's smile widened even more at the compliment and she rubbed the back of her tapered haircut at the thought of Shane thinking that about her. It had been a while since she'd heard—really heard—such things from her own husband. Over the past year when he said them, it made her skin crawl, because it only made her wonder how many times he said that same thing to Raegan. In her mind, that woman would likely always be a part of their relationship somehow. At this point in their strained marriage, she believed that she would always wonder what he did and said to Raegan when they spent time together, no matter how hard they tried to put the past behind them to repair their marriage and heal open wounds. There was no denying that he lied, manipulated and deceived her. The promises they made to each other on their wedding day were now nothing but a heap of shattered vows, likely unrepairable from the damage that had been done.

The ride to the Riverwalk was silent between them at first, with only the music from the radio filling the silence. This was the first time they had been completely alone since the kiss. They'd been spending time in public places where they wouldn't have much privacy and that was probably a good thing. Being alone would likely cause more trouble than they'd bargained for, and the thought of Shane kissing her again tonight made Chloe anxious. As for Shane, he was praying that it would happen again. He wasn't going to apologize for it because he wasn't sorry. Sorry that she was married, sure, but not sorry that he'd gotten a chance to do something that he'd been wanting to do for so long.

Chloe, however, thought to apologize but chose to leave it alone. She thought it was proper to apologize since she was still married, but her heart wouldn't mean it, and her voice would betray her. She enjoyed the kiss and wanted to feel Shane's lips pressed against hers again, but she knew that probably wasn't the best thing for them right now. She kept reminding herself not to bring Shane into her messy life. They didn't need a fourth person in their marriage.

"So, have you heard anything back from the hospital?" Considering they'd known each other most of their lives, Shane thought it was ridiculous that they were acting like strangers or teenagers going on a first date. He had to say something to break the silence.

"Yep!" Chloe sang and smiled, leaving Shane to probe for details.

"And? Did they offer you the position?" *Are you staying or what?* That is what he really wanted to ask. Her staying around gave him a little more hope. That potentially meant that he would get to see her more and spend more time getting to know her again.

"Of course! Looks like I'll be hanging around here for a while." She took note of the glimmer of excitement that Shane had in his eyes after congratulating her. *Kelly is right. I can definitely see this thing that Shane has for me.* She smiled at the thought. It felt good to know that someone was excited about her being around.

Shane took mental note of all the things they could and hopefully would do together since Chloe would be sticking around for at least another two months. That could be good for the two of them.

"So what does Rico think about this? Have you told him?" It was an awkward question but they were friends if nothing else. Shane took his eyes off the road for a split second to note her expression. He was certain that she wasn't expecting that question and her mood shifted from pleasant to irritated.

"Right now, he doesn't get an opportunity to offer his thoughts on anything that I have going on in my life. So, no, I haven't told him and I don't care what he thinks," she snapped.

The way she lifted her left eyebrow and slanted her head to the side told him that the conversation was over. If she were anyone else, he would offer his advice, but this wasn't the time or the place for that. The attitude that she caught when he mentioned her husband told him that their problems ran a little deeper than he realized. And even if he were to get a chance with her, he would likely be the one left with having to undo all of the damage that had been done. It would be a long time to get to the place he really wanted to be with her.

"We're here." Shane motioned to the Riverwalk with a nod of his head. Perfect timing because they needed something to relieve the tension that had been stirred when he asked about her husband.

"This is beautiful," Chloe commented, taking in the scenery as Shane opened her door. She noticed that some people had already claimed their spaces on the lawn with blankets, lawn chairs and coolers. Some adults were near the stage where a band was gearing up to play. She didn't know the band, but most of the people gathered around the stage seemed to know and love them. Children ran around squealing in excitement and playing on the water slides and climbing walls. The scene warmed her heart. That was what she longed for—a family to enjoy occasions like this with.

Shane held out his hand to her and she accepted it. She felt a tiny spark in her heart at the connection. *I shouldn't be feeling that,* she thought. Instead of letting go, she held on a little tighter as he guided her along the riverfront. Although the firework show hadn't started, every now and again, a random firework lit the sky as he showed her around the area. So much had changed since she'd lived there. It was absolutely gorgeous.

Once the crowd started filtering in, Shane went to his truck to grab the blankets.

After he made a pallet on the ground, he sat down and reached out his hand to help Chloe to the spot right next to him. She sat a lot closer to him than he expected, and even though it was nearly one hundred degrees outside and becoming quite crowded, he welcomed her body heat.

They chatted with each other and with families sitting to either side of them until the fireworks started, the band began to play and they were no longer able to hear themselves. They were mesmerized by the beauty of the light show taking place in the sky.

Shane glanced over at Chloe to see the lights dancing in her eyes. "Beautiful," he mouthed close enough to her face that she would hear him but also close enough to kiss. No matter what his intentions were, Chloe closed the gap and pressed her lips against his, relishing the feeling that melted her heart and took her mind away from her problem—Rico.

CHAPTER 17

"Hey! C'mon in, son," an older gentleman called out to Rico as he stood in the doorway to one of the meeting rooms at the church. He had returned to Houston and Pastor Lewis thought that he was right on time to attend a meeting at the church, R.A.S.P., the Reformed Adulterers Support Program, which Pastor Lewis put together for the men who came to him for marital advice. It seemed as if plenty of the men in his church were having trouble being faithful to their wives, and R.A.S.P. became the perfect opportunity to host small group meetings to give spiritual guidance on marriage.

Rico hesitantly entered the room and noticed that each brother sat in a circle holding on to his Bible or tablet. Pastor

Lewis had spoken to Rico a little about the group, but Rico had no idea who would be present. He was actually surprised to see many of the men there, a combination of both young and old, and different races. What surprised him the most was seeing men who he thought had it all together and had beautiful relationships with their wives—perhaps they did because of meeting with the pastor and participating in this group. *Lord, let it work for me too,* Rico thought as he glanced around the room before taking a seat.

He found an open seat next to the former deacon who called out to him when he stood in the doorway, shook hands with a few brothers that he passed getting to his chair, gave an occasional wave and nod of the head to others, took his seat, and avoided eye contact with the group. He didn't bring his Bible because he didn't think this would be some type of Bible study session, but from the looks of things, he figured it might be. He could pull the Bible app up on his phone if he needed to, so he didn't sweat it.

Every second Rico sat in that meeting, he wanted to kick himself for putting himself in that position. But he was there now and he promised himself that he would do whatever it took to win his wife back. He pulled out his phone to send a text to Chloe but decided against it. He hadn't spoken to her since she left and that wasn't the way he wanted to communicate with her the first time he reached out to her. He had to be on his A game, and sending a text message would probably prove just the opposite. He needed everything to be in line when he contacted her, especially since he was certain she didn't want to hear from him at all. He wanted to give her a reason to listen to him and take his love and renewed commitment to her seriously.

"I'm Derek," the gentleman sitting next to him introduced himself and extended his hand to Rico. Rico recognized him because he was formerly on the deacon board, but Rico didn't know anything about him beyond that. Most of the faces in the room were new to him. Each Sunday, about a thousand members went in and out of the sanctuary and Rico didn't really know anyone personally, he only knew faces.

"Oh, I'm sorry man, I'm Rico." He returned the handshake. Derek had rescued him from sinking into the issues that plagued him the moment Chloe pulled out of their driveway.

"So are you here for support to stay in line or are you in the doghouse?"

"Hmph," Rico replied sadly at Derek's comment, and drifted off for a moment, his eyes glazed over. He wished he was in either of those situations. Truth is that he was nowhere near the doghouse. The dog would actually be in better graces with Chloe than he was right now.

"No sir. I need to get her back first," Rico answered, reeling his mind back into the present. He rubbed his hand down the back of his head and rested it on the back of his neck for a moment. The stress from this situation was causing his neck and so many other parts of him to be in pain. He hunched over and hung his head low.

Derek slapped his back and encouraged him when he saw how pathetic Rico looked. "Don't worry, man. You're definitely in the right place. Pastor keeps it real in these sessions. If you do what he says, you'll be on your way to getting your woman back. I can halfway guarantee it," Derek said to cheer him up. He had the voice of a country singer, Rico thought. If he dragged his words out any longer, he'd be singing a country song. The only thing missing would be his guitar. "I guess the other part depends on how badly you messed up and if she is willing to take you back."

"Yeah . . . that's what concerns me," Rico answered, keeping his head low, focusing on the sand-colored ceramic tile floor as if it were speaking to him.

Pastor Lewis walked in and interrupted the different conversations taking place in the room. He exuded confidence, strength and self-control. Rico wondered if he had ever had the problem that he was helping so many men with, but he dared not ask the question.

"Good evening mighty men of God. Let's get right to it. Anybody want to give us an update?" Pastor Lewis clasped his hands together as he took a seat in the circle.

A sharing session? Oh Lord! Rico wondered. He was too embarrassed to share his story, so he hoped that sharing was not a requirement.

Derek raised his hand and announced to the group that he would be the first to share. The gesture made Rico shrink in his seat. He just knew that now all eyes would be on him. Even though he wasn't the one talking, he was the *new* guy to the group and everyone was sure to notice that he was sitting next to the man who currently had the floor.

"Jackie and I are stronger than ever these days. I just have to give God praise because there was a time when I thought we would never mend our marriage, but to be in the place we're in now is pure evidence that there is a God and that He has shown me favor," Derek began with that country drawl. Derek glanced at Rico before continuing to share more of his story. "And since there are some brothers here that don't know my story, I would like to share it in hopes that it might provide some encouragement for those who think their situation is hopeless. Is that all right, Pastor?" Derek asked, his voice deep and country. Rico was certain he was from some part of Mississippi. Pastor Lewis nodded his agreement and Derek continued.

"You see, I had an affair with my secretary for eight months. It started off as compliments between the two of us, then progressed to lunch dates, then to working late hours. But check this out. It was gradual. It kinda snuck up on me. I wasn't looking to have an affair, but because I was spending all of this time with her, emotions somehow jumped in. The first time I cheated on my wife, we hadn't had sex in about three months. I didn't find out until later that she believed she was unattractive to me because she had gained about fifteen pounds. So she didn't want me to see her naked. And her standoffish attitude made me think that she wasn't attracted to me anymore.

"Jessica started giving me all the attention that I wanted my wife to give me, and that tiny spark between us became a flame. I never knew how my wife felt until we had our counseling sessions with Pastor here. It's just a shame that it took an affair to get us to communicate like a husband and wife should. When I took those vows with her twenty years ago, I meant every word of it, and I still intend to keep them today.

"There were some hurt feelings," Derek continued. "There were some tears and some ugly truths, but we dealt with it and now we're closer than we've ever been. We talk about every issue, even if we know it's going to make us uncomfortable, and that's the way it has to be, brothers. We can't be afraid to let these women in. Remember that they loved us enough to choose to be with us forever. The least that we can do is to show them that they didn't make a stupid choice." Derek laughed and slapped Rico on the shoulder again.

Rico knew that most of that speech was for him. Even after they starting counseling, there were still a lot of things left unsaid between him and Chloe. If he could just take it all back, he would.

"Thank you for sharing that, Brother Derek," Pastor Lewis said. "And that is sort of what I want us to focus on tonight, *Loving our wives as ourselves,"* Pastor began as he opened his Bible and started a lesson from Ephesians 5:25. The group followed by opening their Bibles and taking out pens and paper. "The Word of God teaches us to put our wives first by loving them as we love ourselves. Just think of this. Before you were married, didn't you put your needs first?" Pastor Lewis paused for discussion before continuing, "Now that you are married, you are to love your wife as yourself. The problem that most of us have is that we show love the way we want to be loved, and we often go wrong there. We have to love them the way they want and need to be loved. What is it that makes your wife feel like she's loved by you? If you don't know the answer, then that is your assignment for this week. Find out what makes her feel loved and do something to love her in that way. I'm looking forward to hearing the reports from this."

A couple of them chatted about their wives and what they'd done in the past to show love. Flowers. Candy. Gifts. Date nights. But none of them knew exactly what their wife's response would be to the pastor's question. Including Rico. He figured if he knew the answer to that question, he would have loved her the way she needed and probably wouldn't be sitting in that room. He'd tried the traditional flowers and jewelry to say *I'm sorry,* but that didn't make things all better; in fact, it probably made it worse. Chloe despised receiving tangible gifts to make up for wrongs because she felt like he was trying to buy his way out of hurting her; she needed to see action and Rico had failed to act in such a way that would help her trust him again.

Pastor Lewis dismissed them after ending their session with a word of prayer. Rico lagged behind to thank him for the invitation. He didn't necessarily receive any answers as to how he would get Chloe back, but he had a feeling that being a part of R.A.S.P. would be a great start.

"Thanks, Pastor. I think I needed this. Well, I take that back, I know I did," Rico said, standing next to Pastor Lewis with his hands stuffed inside his pockets and his shoulders slightly slumped. Something about being a part of that meeting brought a sense of humility within him. He didn't have it all together, but a lot of others didn't either. He felt like he was in the right place to get just the help he needed. And the best thing of all is that he believed that God would help him. For that, he was thankful and expecting things to change in his life.

"No problem, son. I see some of myself in you, and I want nothing more than to save our marriages. If there was something I could do for all married couples over the world to help them stay together, I would," Pastor Lewis said and proceeded to quote divorce rates. Pastor and Rico stacked the last of the chairs while finishing their conversation.

"Well, let me be the one to say that what you're doing here, sir, is a great start. Before I go, I do have a question for you," Rico said, confusion plastered across his face as he stacked the last chair.

Pastor Lewis nodded.

"How am I going to complete the assignment if my wife isn't here?"

Pastor Lewis smiled. "That is the fun part, isn't it? God bless you, brother," he answered, slapping Rico across the shoulder and walked away, leaving Rico in the empty room to wonder how he would go about completing his assignment.

Don't give up on me just yet, Chloe. I've got a plan.

CHAPTER 18

Shane's lips felt so good against hers. All it took was for Chloe to think about the time he kissed her during the fireworks show or after their trip to the museum or the moment they never spoke of that happened way back when. It didn't necessarily matter which kiss, they all caused her to feel flutters in her heart that she should only feel for her husband. And although it wasn't quite right, it surely felt right in the moment.

Maybe Rico needs to know exactly what it feels like to be me, she mused. But she wasn't Rico and even as she thought about taking things a step further with Shane she could hear her mother's voice preaching to her. *"Turn the other cheek." Ha! Easy for her to say,* Chloe thought.

"CeCe!" Shane called out to Chloe. She had been sitting on a bench in the park waiting for him to meet her. She arrived early to give herself time to think. Something about being in the midst of God's creation, coupled with the smell of fresh air and the gentle breeze, often helped infuse a calmness in her and allowed her to clear her mind. Today it didn't work. She whipped her head around at his voice. He hadn't called her that since high school. No one had.

"CeCe? You went way back, huh?" She chuckled softly and stood to greet him.

"Seemed appropriate." He smiled and pulled her into a hug. "You look and smell great. How are you today?"

"I'm good. Come sit for a moment." Chloe returned to the bench and patted the empty spot next to her. She hadn't seen him in his uniform since the day he pulled her over. He was even more handsome than she remembered.

Chloe thought that today was as good a time as any to bring up the recent kisses they shared. They hadn't acknowledged the kiss outside the museum except with another one at the fireworks show.

"What's up?" Shane asked after sitting down and relaxing next to her, crossing one leg over the other while stretching one arm across the back of the bench behind her.

"I think we should talk about what's going on with us," she began. "I enjoy spending time with you, but not in the way we did when we were younger. I have to be honest with both myself and you, and I think I'm developing feelings for you . . . and I don't think I should be. Even after everything that Rico has done, I'm still married to him. You do understand that, right?" Chloe finished, staring ahead. She didn't want to see what she thought would be the look of disappointment in his eyes. They both sat watching kids run around on the playground, residents walk their dogs and others power walk around the trail surrounding the park.

Shane ground his teeth together and thought for a moment. He knew this conversation was coming and he had dreaded hearing the whole *You're a great guy but* speech again. He was fully aware that Chloe was still married and he wasn't expecting any sort of commitment from her, but she had to know that he believed she was special—made especially for him.

"I understand but you have to know that—" Shane's near confession was cut off by the voice coming from his radio. There was a robbery nearby, and although he wasn't on the clock yet, duty called. He jumped up from the bench and gave her a quick peck on the cheek. "See, that's appropriate, right? Just want you to know I heard you." He winked and left in pursuit of the burglars.

Shane was only six blocks away when he hopped into his patrol car and responded to the call, alerting dispatch that he was in pursuit. Four blocks down the street, he saw the suspects running away on foot. When he saw the two men, dressed in blue sweatshirts, black ski masks, and black pants, run near an alley, he pulled over and continued his pursuit on foot.

"If I don't catch them, they are sure to pass out from this heat, wearing sweatshirts and it's near one hundred degrees outside," he huffed as he chased the two men. One of them turned to see Shane gaining on them. The other one shouted, "Hey man, c'mon! You're slowing down us down, looking back at every turn."

Because of a previous knee injury, Shane was not prepared to jump the fence they came upon, and one of the men made sure he didn't get over it. The smaller one turned and revealed a gun. As Shane reacted to reach for his weapon, he felt a pain in his chest that stung so deeply, he barely had enough time to call for backup before he blacked out against the pavement.

"Officer down . . . help . . . now," he said between short, ragged breaths before passing out.

"Look at what you've done. Idiot! Now why did you have to shoot him! You're on your own! Stupid!" the other man cursed as he split up from the shooter. He was a thief but definitely not a killer.

∞

"Chloe! Get in here!" Kelly yelled into the kitchen from the living room. Kelly sat on the couch, legs folded under her, sipping her chai tea latte. When Chloe walked in the room, Kelly sent her children upstairs and pointed at the TV as the news anchor discussed breaking news.

When Chloe saw the news of an officer shooting flashing at the bottom of the TV screen, she clutched her chest and plopped down on the couch to listen to the anchorman. The shooting took place not far from the park she visited earlier. No wonder she hadn't heard from Shane; it had to be him, she concluded, although the news anchor did not mention an officer's name.

"I have to go to the hospital. I can't leave him there by himself." Chloe stood to grab her purse and keys when the story ended. She tried calling his phone but didn't receive an answer. She had to go find out if it was him or not.

"Go." As much as Kelly believed that her sister should be keeping her distance from Shane, she had a heart. She couldn't be the one to tell her to let Shane's family take care of him. Shane was like family to them since they grew up as close neighbors. She wanted Shane to be all right, too.

"None of this is helping her deal with her marital issues," Kelly said to herself before taking a sip of tea, watching her sister walk out of the door to check up on the man who seemed to be winning her heart.

CHAPTER 19

Rico fiddled with his cell phone for nearly an hour before he gathered the nerve to call his wife. The house was quiet, no TV or radio, and the only sound he heard was his nervous, uneven breathing. He sat on the second to the last step of the staircase and took deep breaths as he rehearsed every possible scenario and attempted to come up with a reaction for how she might respond to his call.

He started to dial her number but placed the phone on the step in between his feet and did something he hadn't done in a while—prayed before taking action.

"God, I know that if there is anyone who can help me in all of this it's You. I know I haven't been faithful and I don't deserve anything from You, but if You will, please soften Chloe's heart and cause her to give me another chance. That's all I want. Please God. Thanks. Amen."

Rico felt like he hadn't spent enough time with God to be asking things of Him, but he needed this. Hoping that God heard him and would act immediately, he picked up the phone, and with trembling fingers, held down the number 1 to speed dial Chloe. He was already preparing for her voicemail to pick up when he heard the line open and her voice on the other end of the phone.

"Yes, hello," she answered. Her voice held no emotion. He assumed that she was still holding onto everything that he'd done. But she at least answered the phone, so that was progress.

"Hey, you were on my mind, so I just wanted to check on you to see how you're doing. Everything all right?" Rico asked and held his breath for a response.

"Yes." Hearing his voice on the line was bittersweet. She felt a smile creeping across her lips, but it was quickly replaced by a scowl at the thought of him just *calling to check in on Raegan.* She wondered if that's how things got started between the two of them.

For a moment, there was silence on the line. Chloe didn't add anything to her response; she wasn't offering any additional information. She was doing good to answer his call.

"Look, Rico, if you didn't want anything, I need to go. I'm kinda in the middle of something," she said as she searched the hospital garage for a parking space. She had to find out if Shane was the officer who had been shot.

"Oh. I didn't want to bother you. I just wanted you to know that you were on my mind. You in town?"

"I'm not," Chloe said dryly, again, offering no additional information, leaving Rico to wonder.

"Can we meet when you come back?" Rico asked, trying to get a feel for when she'd return to Houston. Based on the dry conversation they were having, he knew that was a long shot. He would have to ask specific questions if he wanted specific answers.

"I don't know if I'm ready for that yet or if I'm ever coming back." Chloe surprised herself with that answer. It wasn't until now that she actually seriously considered staying in Nashville. There was really nothing for her in Houston anymore. She enjoyed working at the hospital in Nashville and was certain she could find a permanent position. *And spend more time with Shane,* she thought.

"I see, well just let me know. I really want to see you. And Chloe?"

"Yeah?"

"Don't give up on me just yet; I still love you." He wasn't expecting a profession of love from her, but he wanted her to know where he stood. He fully intended to get things back on track with their marriage, and this was the beginning of his best foot forward.

Just as he expected, silence met his declaration. It wasn't as if Chloe wasn't glad to hear that her husband loved her, it was that she didn't believe him. Or maybe he didn't know what it meant to love a wife. It surely didn't mean to sleep with and create a baby with another woman.

"I have to go. Bye." Chloe ended the call. She paused before getting out of the car to rush into the emergency room. "What was that about?"

Rico hadn't contacted her since she left. Why was he calling her now?

∞

Rico stared at his phone's home screen for a moment. It wasn't as bad as it could have been, but not as good as he'd hoped for either. He wanted to at least talk to her about something that he'd done in the past to make her feel loved so that he could complete his assignment. But it didn't seem like the right time to have that conversation. He was certain she would have thought that he was losing his mind. For all he knew, his infidelity had clouded her mind and she couldn't even bring herself to think about him making her feel loved and appreciated. Another hurdle that he would have to cross to get her back. The more he thought about it, the more he realized how badly he had messed up. *Just how am I going to get us out of this mess?* he wondered. If he didn't know it before, he now knew that he had a long way to go before Chloe would see him as the man she married years ago.

∞

Chloe gathered her composure and walked into the emergency room. She saw a group of about five officers standing in a huddle and knew they had to be there for Shane. As she inched closer, she recognized one of them, David, who went to school with her and Shane.

"David! Hey! Is Shane all right?" She didn't have confirmation that Shane was the officer shot but was grateful to see David and have him be the one to confirm or deny her suspicion.

"Chloe? Woman, I thought you were never coming back to this place!" He pulled her into a tight hug, slightly lifting her off her feet. "It's so good to see you! Shane is going to be fine. The doctors were able to get the bullet out. It wasn't as bad as they initially thought when they brought him in."

"Oh, thank God!" she exclaimed, clutching her chest. Her intuition was right. She hated that Shane was the one shot, but was relieved to hear that he was expected to pull through just fine. "I want to see him. Are they allowing him to have visitors yet?"

"We're all waiting. Just hang around here. Hey guys, this is Chloe. Chloe meet Mark, Devin, Michael and Jeff."

Chloe shook each of their hands and remained standing in their circle, listening to them share stories about Shane. Seemed as if this wasn't his first time taking a bullet and Chloe didn't like the sound of that one bit.

About two hours later, Shane was moved to a recovery room and allowed visitors. "Ladies first," the officers all said and gestured for her to be the first person to see Shane.

"Is it true that you regularly take bullets, Superman Cop?" Chloe half-joked when she entered the room.

Shane chuckled and then winced from the pain.

"I suppose that David and some of the guys are out there talking about me. It was only one other time. Does this mean you're worried about me, *friend*?"

"Of course I am! Imagine how freaked out I was when I heard about this on the news. You know they never leave you with an ounce of hope! I was scared to death to think that you were the officer shot. I'm so glad you're all right. How are you feeling?" she asked, inching closer to his bedside.

"Much better now. My best friend in the whole world came to see me," he answered and grinned, putting emphasis on the word *friend* again.

Chloe hugged him when she made it to his side. That hug was much better than any kiss she'd ever shared with him because he was alive. She had come too close to losing him.

"Too bad we're only friends. I could use a kiss right now. You know kisses make everything better, right?" Shane teased.

Chloe snickered and planted a soft kiss on his temple. "All better."

"Much better. You don't know how much I appreciate you coming to check up on me. Thank you,," he said, pulling her hands to his lips to brush them with a kiss. He sounded a lot better than she'd expected, considering he had just been shot and was recovering from surgery.

"No problem at all. Isn't that what friends do?" She winked and smiled. Sitting in the chair next to the bed, she eyed him carefully after staring at the dressings covering his wound. Her mood became serious once again as the realization set in that he could have died. Why did he have to have such a dangerous career? She knew it had to be done, but why him?

"Hey," Shane interrupted her thoughts and rubbed his hand along her arm. "It's okay. Protect and serve, remember? That's what I do. I don't worry much because I know that God is going to protect me. It is only by His grace that I am sitting in this hospital bed and not in the morgue."

"Yea, you're right . . . so when are you getting out of here?"

"Tomorrow. I know you're going to miss me, but I'll be fine." They both burst into laughter at the comment. True she would miss him, but she knew where to find him if she needed him.

"Your cop friends are waiting outside to see you, so I'm going to go back to Kelly's. There was no way I would've been able to get any rest tonight until I knew if you were all right. I've seen you for myself, so I'm satisfied now."

"Thanks for caring so much." His eyes were filled with emotion and words left unsaid.

Chloe got up to leave and Shane pulled her in for another hug. When she pulled away, he gave her a lingering look.

"How much longer are you here? I won't waste my time recovering if you're thinking of leaving town soon."

"Much longer than anticipated. I'm going to start looking for my own place. Kelly's husband is returning from overseas soon. I'm sure they'll need some time alone without me hanging around there like a third wheel."

"Oh, so does getting your own place mean that Nashville is gonna become your permanent place of residence?" His eyebrows rose playfully, but he was hopeful.

"I guess we'll have to wait and see, won't we?" she said as she backed toward the door.

Shane put his hands together as if he were about to pray and bowed his head. He mouthed "thank you" and winked at her as she left the room. Things were starting to look better and better for him. If she was staying, that could only mean one thing: she was leaving Rico.

CHAPTER 20

Two days later, after Shane had been released from the hospital, Chloe stopped by his place to check in on him and take him food. She thought that was the kind thing to do since he was her friend and she cared for him. Before going, she toyed with the idea for a while, trying to convince herself that she wasn't crossing any boundaries. She didn't want to be just as guilty as Rico. She decided that this was completely different. Shane needed her right now and her intentions were pure.

"Thank you for volunteering to be my nurse," Shane said after producing a fake cough.

"For one, you can stop pretending to have a cough . . . that isn't why I'm here. And two, have you forgotten that I am a nurse and it's my duty to care for the sick? Besides, I've practically known you my whole life; I'm almost obligated to come see about you." Chloe fluffed pillows and made sure that Shane was positioned comfortably on the couch.

Shane playfully tagged her with a pillow as she walked away from the couch after checking his bandages. He was going to be just fine and she was thankful to God for that. Almost losing him made her realize that she cared more about him than she thought and far more than as the boy who grew up next door to her.

Chloe made sure he was comfortable and had everything he needed, including lunch that she prepared for him.

"All right dude, I'm outta here. My shift starts in about an hour. I'll check on you periodically to make sure you're good. Okay?" She leaned over the couch, planted a kiss on his forehead and whispered a silent prayer for his health. She couldn't have him clocking out on her while she was at work, although she had faith that he would be just fine since he received the doctor's okay to be released from the hospital.

Before she could fully stand to walk away, he tugged her hand and pulled her in closer to him so that he could thank her with a kiss. She smiled, nodded and walked away to keep from giving in to her desire to kiss him back, much more passionately than he'd kissed her.

She grabbed her purse and keys and walked out the door rubbing her fingers against her lips. She could still feel his lips pressed up against hers. *This is becoming a thing,* she thought as she made her way to the car.

Before starting the car, she glanced at Shane's house for a moment and then back to her reflection in the sun-visor mirror. Chloe never thought she'd be giving up on her marriage, but she'd thought about it even more since Rico's call a few days ago. She felt more contempt in her heart than love at the sound of his voice. For the sake of her marriage, she wanted to get past what he did to her, but she knew she couldn't. She opened her purse and pulled out the documents she'd been carrying around for the past several weeks. If she were to be completely honest with herself, there was only one thing left to do—send the divorce papers.

CHAPTER 21

As much as Kelly wished that Chloe's marriage could be saved, she wasn't on Rico's side. For hurting her sister, she wanted to give him a piece of her mind—and Rico being on the other end of the phone had her insides boiling. It was as if he was begging for her to let loose the pent-up anger she felt towards him.

"Please talk to your sister for me. I love her and I need her here at home with me. C'mon, I'm begging you, Kelly," Rico's voice cracked a little as he pleaded with her to fight on his behalf.

"I'm not sure what I can do for you. Why don't you call her yourself? That's a start." Kelly really wanted to curse him out, but she resisted by reminding herself that it was Chloe's battle, not hers.

Just when she was starting to feel sorry for him, Rico let out an exasperated sigh, as if Kelly was the one doing something wrong. Even if that isn't how he meant it, that's exactly how she took it.

"Now you hold on one minute! Don't forget that you're the one who got yourself into this mess! Slangin' your man thang all over Houston—so you can keep your attitude in check brotha!" Kelly spewed, this time without holding her tongue.

He had some nerve trying to make his problems her problems. If it were possible, she would reach through the phone and wring his neck for Chloe. That wouldn't be Christ-like but it would sure make her and her sister feel better, even if it was temporary satisfaction.

Rico inhaled deeply, not only taking in oxygen but Kelly's words. Although true, they stung deeply. If he were to be honest, his issues with Chloe started long before Raegan, but he wanted his wife back and Kelly was the one person he knew who could influence Chloe on his behalf. He knew he needed to be kind to her.

"I'm sorry. For real, I am. It just seems like life is constantly beating me down right now, just as I'm trying to get things back on track," Rico continued, listing off everything he was doing as if he had a checklist and that list was what he needed to turn his life around. "I'm back in church . . . I've even started volunteering as an usher twice a month. I'm praying more and reading my Bible. And now I'm having health issues and it seems as if my wife is pulling further and further away," Rico lamented. His heart was heavy and there was a ringing in his ears much like that of a train whistle.

"Will you please just tell her to come home and work this out?" Rico pleaded once more, his voice cracking. He stared at the wrinkled-up divorce papers lying on the coffee table in front of him. He didn't mention that to Kelly because he wasn't sure if she knew about that yet or if mentioning it would help his case. All he knew was that he was determined not to sign anything that would officially end their marriage. The moment he received them, he crushed them and tossed them to the floor, taking his anger out on sheets of paper as if that would solve his problems. He had a feeling that they may have been coming, but he thought he had a little more time. Time was constantly proving not to be on his side.

"Listen Rico. I want my sister to live in peace and happiness, and if that's with you, then fine, but I don't want to be in the middle of this, so please don't pull me in. This isn't my battle to fight. You do know that, right?" Her question was a reminder to both him and herself. When Rico didn't respond, she said reluctantly, "But I will do you this one favor and talk to her. The rest is up to you." She sighed and rolled her eyes heavenward. If she were to be real with herself, she was already in the middle of it, constantly in Chloe's ear to remind her that she was still married. And not only that, Kelly was doing her best to encourage

Chloe to keep Shane out of this. From the looks of things, it might even be too late for that. And now here she was again, getting in the middle of it by agreeing to go to Chloe on Rico's behalf. What a mess.

"Appreciate that Kels. Have a good day," Rico said and ended the call, somewhat satisfied that Kelly would talk to Chloe for him. He picked up the divorce papers and eased them into the shredder, page by page. Shredding the papers did nothing to help his case, because if he went too long without either signing or contesting, she would likely get a chance to proceed with the divorce anyway.

"If she wants this divorce, she's gonna have to come get it," Rico vowed confidently as the machine ground the last page. Something about destroying the divorce papers gave him a boost in confidence, especially after he nearly lost it when her lawyer served him. He was ready to fight, and he hoped that by not signing the divorce papers, she would see the fight in him, recognize his newfound commitment and reconsider the divorce. She had to know just how dedicated he was to making their marriage work again; he only hoped that she would commit to rebuilding their marriage as well.

After turning off the shredder, he stretched out on the sofa and relaxed his head on the pillow. Who would have thought that a string of doctor visits over the last several weeks would result in him finding out that he had prostate cancer. He didn't mention it to

Kelly because he didn't want Chloe running back to him because of an illness; he wanted her to want him and their marriage. He closed his eyes in an effort to fight the tears that threatened to slide down his cheeks. *Is this my punishment, God? If so, I'll take it, but please send Chloe back to me,* Rico thought. No wife. No mistress. No baby. Just cancer. That was all he had. His life couldn't get any worse.

CHAPTER 22

Before Chloe could make it into her sister's house and get comfortable, Kelly had to mention Rico, immediately putting a damper on Chloe's mood. As much as she tried to put Rico's infidelity out of her mind and enjoy the little bit of happiness she was experiencing, she couldn't because Kelly took every opportunity to remind her that she was still married to an adulterer, whom she needed to decide if she was going to stay married to. The decision had already been made and Kelly was aware of that fact. She had God and the Texas law on her side. Knowing that her lawyer had filed the papers on her behalf and served Rico gave her an unexplainable amount of peace. So why Kelly would even entertain Rico, she had no idea.

Kelly hoped that it would change things a little for Chloe to learn that Rico had been calling and asking about her, so Kelly brought up her recent conversation with him. She felt bad for the guy and for her sister, but she wanted them to be happy—together or not. That was definitely not the news that Chloe was expecting. Her smile was replaced with a frown, crinkled eyebrows and somewhat of an attitude. She rolled her eyes and plopped down on the sofa next to Kelly, hardly acknowledging her comments about their telephone conversation, other than the scowl on her face.

"So you're really prepared to end your marriage, Chloe?" Kelly argued when she didn't receive the type of response she was expecting after sharing that Rico called practically begging Kelly to help him get his wife back.

Chloe was glad that she had finally moved into her own place because she wouldn't be able to stand her sister defending Rico at every turn, like him pleading with Kelly was going to magically make everything okay.

"I love you, Kelly, and I know what you're trying to do, but you can't be seriously advocating for this marriage!" Chloe jumped up and began pacing. "It was over the moment Rico stepped out on me—twice! And you're not in my shoes either. Are you sure you'd be singing the same song if your hubby went out and started another family behind your back?" Chloe halted a moment and gave her sister a doubtful look, raising an eyebrow.

"You're right, I don't know, but we're talking about you. Does this have anything to do with your feelings for Shane?" Kelly's question infuriated Chloe even more.

"Let's not forget that Shane was nowhere around when Rico was gallivanting around town sniffing under someone else's skirt," Chloe reminded Kelly, her voice raised a couple of octaves, clearly appalled that she would bring Shane into this. Whatever her feelings were for Shane, they had nothing to do with her disgust for Rico.

Kelly couldn't help but burst into laughter at Chloe's remark. That sounded exactly like something their mother would say. Though Chloe hated to admit it, she was a lot like their mom in many ways. Her using the word *gallivanting* was proof of it.

Chloe erupted into laughter as well, lightening the moment, and changing the subject to all of the funny things their mother would say. Chloe wondered how her mother would have handled the situation. Though her mother's speech was filled with country twang, her mother was poised and proper. Even if their father did cheat, her mother would probably stay with him to save face. At least that is what Chloe imagined would happen.

Chloe reclaimed her seat on the couch after she'd calmed down and linked arms with Kelly. Chloe rested her head on Kelly's shoulder and tears began to slowly roll down her cheeks as the realization of what she'd decided to do set in.

"Kel, it's not like I didn't try. Before I came out here, I spent the last year trying my best to make things work. Well, I can't say 'make them work.' More like trying to get over what he did to me. It's hard. The more I try, the more thoughts of him and the other woman continue to creep up in my mind. I don't know if I'll ever be able to get over it," Chloe admitted through broken sobs.

Kelly wanted to tell her that time heals all wounds, but that probably wasn't the best choice of words to encourage her; so she rubbed her sister's arm and listened. She knew it was a lot for her to handle and was sorry she was going through it. If she could take the pain away, she would, but that was an obstacle that Chloe would have to work through.

Kelly debated whether or not to tell Chloe more about her conversation with Rico earlier that day. He seemed pretty shaken up. He shared with her his involvement in the men's group at church and how he was working on getting himself right with the Lord so that he could be the man that Chloe needed him to be. He just needed Chloe to give him more time. Give their relationship more time. He planned to fight for them, and she was certain that giving up on their marriage was the farthest thing from his mind. She'd save that conversation for a later day, if Chloe would even hear of it.

The one person that she could count on who had more wisdom than she did was their mother. Chloe wouldn't be happy about it, but she had had to call her. Hearing the faint sound of the car engine shutting off, Kelly unlinked their arms, stood up and walked to the door.

"Please don't be mad," Kelly pleaded as she opened the door.

"What?" Confusion clouded Chloe's eyes as she dabbed her cheeks. In a half-second, Chloe realized there was only one reason Kelly would say that.

"I had to . . . Momma! You look cute!"

"Honey, 'cute' is for lil' girls. Just say it, I'm fine." Their mother entered the house and twirled to show off her new summer sheath dress.

"Hey Ma." Chloe walked over to greet her with a huge, lingering hug. It had been several months since she'd last seen her parents, and even though she knew her mother would chew her out about her decision, she still needed her mother's touch.

"Rico looked pretty pitiful when I saw him in Alabama. What's going on? Did you leave him for good?" Their mother got straight to the point as she sauntered into the house and made herself comfortable.

Chloe couldn't quite make out if her mother already knew the answer to her own question or if she really had no clue about what was going on.

"Got one foot out the door. He got served last week," Chloe answered casually. "I'm surprised that Kelly didn't fill you in."

Kelly shot her mother a look as if to say "don't you dare tell her I told you." She didn't want her sister thinking that she betrayed her confidence, but she needed backup.

"Figures," Chloe grunted, noticing the nonverbal exchange between the two of them.

Ignoring Chloe's comment, her mother continued her probing, asking what happened that would warrant a divorce. The trio walked over to the sofa and lounge chair as Chloe recalled all the details from when she found out about Rico's second affair to her ending up visiting Nashville, even though she was pretty certain that her mother knew everything already. She even shared the thing that hurt the most—the baby he almost had.

"So you made him give the baby up?" her mother asked, genuinely interested as if she was hearing the story for the first time. And in fact she was. Contrary to Chloe's belief, Kelly didn't share all of the details; she only gave her a brief summary— enough to get her to come over and share the kind of wisdom that only a mother could provide. And neither did Rico, when she spoke to him back in Alabama.

"I didn't make him. He signed over his parental because the mistress wanted him to. I'm sure he thought that would make me happy, but what would make me happy is if he hadn't went out and created a baby with her in the first place," Chloe snarled. Her blood was beginning to boil again at the thought of Rico's deceit.

"And now the baby is gone?"

"Yeah, she lost the baby that evening. She was involved in a car accident shortly after all of this happened." Chloe's heart broke all over again. Although a part of her slightly despised Raegan for sleeping with her husband and giving him what Chloe hadn't given him, she still didn't wish any harm to her or the baby she was carrying. She paused for a moment and grabbed her nose. It was starting to sting from the emotion she now felt.

"That's so sad. But what's done is done. The question becomes what are you going to do about it now?" Her mother moved next to her to console her.

"Umm . . . I sent him divorce papers." Chloe thought that she had already made her decision clear earlier in the conversation.

"I see."

"And that's all you have to say?" Chloe asked, clearly confused that her mother didn't start ranting about how she should stay with her husband. Her mother sat up and rubbed her hands down her dress. There was the poised woman that Chloe knew. She braced herself for what she would say next.

"Forgiveness is hard, sweetheart, and if your father had never forgiven me, we wouldn't be together today."

Chloe's and Kelly's heads snapped around at their mother and she simply nodded. She had cheated on their father early in their marriage. Although he forgave her, to this day she still had a hard time forgiving herself.

CHAPTER 23

"How could you do that to Daddy?" Chloe shrieked. She wanted to leave, but the revelation that her mother was an adulterer warranted her staying a bit longer; she needed answers. Her parents must have had some kind of secret and she was anxious to find out what it was. Seeing as though she couldn't get past Rico's infidelity, she couldn't imagine what would make her father stay with her mother.

Cynthia took a sip of tea and closed her eyes, remembering that time in her marriage when she had almost given up everything. There was a long moment of silence before she spoke, and neither of her daughters dared say a word because they both wanted answers. Where did the strength to tough it out come from?

"When your father and I first married, he was in graduate school and working both a full-time and part-time job to make sure ends could meet. I was lonely and just as frustrated as any wife would be if her husband didn't make time for her." She paused and took another sip of tea before continuing.

"Some women would say that I was selfish, but I wanted what I wanted and that was my husband. You two already know that your father isn't the best when it comes to managing his time. I was of the opinion that he could at least set aside an hour for me each day, but I was lucky if I got that in one week."

Kelly and Chloe gave her questioning looks, but she answered their unasked questions.

"I didn't just run off and cheat, of course, I'm not that silly. Eventually, I found myself a hobby." Their mother stood up and walked out of the living room area as if the conversation was finished.

"What is wrong with your mother?" Chloe asked. "I hope she knows that this isn't the end of this little talk. I want to know what happened. I want the whole story. You? Or have you heard this already?" Chloe asked, her voice filled with a hint of suspicion.

Kelly tossed a pillow in Chloe's direction. "Silly, this is my first time hearing this too. Maybe she just needs a moment. Let's give her a minute to come back," Kelly said, resisting the urge to chase their mother through the house, demanding more of an explanation.

Kelly and Chloe waited patiently and silently for their mother to return. She sauntered back into the room a few moments later with another cup of tea, smiled half-heartedly and took her seat.

"Your hobby? The guy you cheated with?" Chloe pushed and gestured for her mother to finish her story.

"Tennis. I started taking tennis lessons to give me something else to do while your father worked, studied or went to class."

"Did you cheat with your tennis instructor?" Kelly interrupted.

"No, my instructor was a woman. Remember, we were having a tough enough time making ends meet, so we couldn't afford to spend too much on these lessons. My instructor was a college student—Jocelyn. It was her older brother, Robert, who I became fond of. He would stop by and watch us play and offer tips and tricks. Pretty soon, he was the one giving more instruction to me than she was."

Cynthia recalled how she and Robert started spending time together without Jocelyn, and their relationship bloomed from there. Her husband was so busy that he didn't notice when or how long she was out of the house, as long as she'd taken care of her wifely and household duties.

Their relationship continued right up until their father graduated. Cynthia's heart had always been with her husband and she thought that Robert understood that she was only passing the time with him. But she was wrong. By the time Cynthia wanted to end things with Robert, he was ready to marry her. He had only been seeing her for about nine months, but had professed his love for her and his desire to spend the rest of his life with her. He wanted her to leave her husband, but that was never an option for Cynthia.

"Robert had become irrational and threatened to tell your father everything if I didn't end my marriage, so I confessed," Cynthia recalled, fingering the pearls around her neck and gazing off into space as she rehashed the story. "I told him about the affair with Robert, every single detail, and how Robert threatened to tell him if I didn't leave him. He was ready to pack his things and leave me, but his love for God and me made him think twice about his decision." Cynthia wiped away at a stray tear before continuing.

"It took us years to work through it, but we were committed to making our marriage work. In fact, he would hardly even look at me or sleep in the same bed for at least six months. And it took him a year before he would even touch me again, because the pain he felt from the thought of another man touching me was just too much for him to bear. But we prayed together about it, through *much* pain and *many, many* tears. That was a turning point in our marriage and helped us grow up when we decided to go before God together in prayer. Neither of us would allow the other to bear the burden alone. I knew the hurt that I caused him and how I destroyed our relationship, but I was *not* giving up without a fight. I absolutely refused. We slowly but surely picked up the pieces together," Cynthia shared, exhaling deeply when she finished.

"I'm glad you guys were able to work through it, because you have a beautiful relationship now," Kelly said as she leaned over to hug her mother, all the while eyeing Chloe. She was thankful that their mother had shared her story with them and hoped that Chloe could learn something from it; her marriage could possibly work too if she was willing to fight for it. Though Kelly halfway despised Rico for the pain he caused, she wondered if knowing their mother had been in a similar situation would compel Chloe to rethink her decision to file for divorce.

"Thank you baby, but the lesson in that was that we loved each other enough to work through it. Every day it is a choice. We choose to be together because we believe that God put us together for a purpose."

Chloe didn't say anything. She only listened and watched the display of affection between her mother and sister from across the room. She considered everything her mother said and mentally she congratulated her on being able to work through it. More so, she congratulated her father for being strong and forgiving enough to take her back. But as for her, in this moment, she wasn't strong enough to deal with things between her and Rico the way her parents did. It hurt far too much. And it took even more out of her not to despise her mother for inflicting the same kind of pain on her father as Rico did on her. She said her good-byes and left; she didn't have it in her to be in the same room with her mother at that moment. As far as she was concerned, her mother was the female version of Rico, and that didn't do either of them any good.

CHAPTER 24

"I look like a pauper compared to you. You're all jazzed up and I'm still in my uniform. You are gorgeous," Shane commented to Chloe as he drove to the restaurant. Chloe was dolled up in a yellow strapless maxi dress and a sheer white shrug. She'd paid a visit to her sister's hair stylist and manicurist earlier that day so that she could look her best. She was giddy about spending time with Shane since they were going on their first *real* date after establishing that there was something between the two of them. Given the circumstances, they decided to take things slow and simply enjoy each other's company, not really sure where it might lead. However, Chloe still wanted to look her best. It had been a while since she felt adored and that made her feel beautiful; she wanted to glow on the outside, just as she did inwardly.

Chloe's cheeks hurt a little from smiling so hard. She hadn't been this happy in a long time. If things were different, Rico would have been the one putting the smile on her face, but he wasn't. Life had no eraser and there was no changing what happened between them or how she felt about it. Right now, she was living in the moment, a moment that she refused to let her issues with Rico be a part of. "Thank you, again. So where are we going?"

"You'll see when we get there. You'll be surprised that this place is still around. We both enjoyed this spot growing up." His eyes lit up thinking about the times they shared as teenagers. He hoped that could be something they could build on.

Chloe rode patiently in the passenger seat, fidgeting with the seatbelt from time to time. She took note of the neighborhoods they drove through, trying to prick her memory, but nothing rang a bell. She figured he must have been trying to take the scenic route or throw her off by turning down all of these random streets.

"So tell me, exactly why are you still in your uniform? *You* asked *me* out; shouldn't you have been more prepared?" Chloe teased.

"Yeah, you're right. Things got a little crazy before my shift ended today and I had to stay a little longer. I'd been thinking about this moment all day and I didn't want to be late getting to you just because of a need to change clothes. It's no biggie, unless you mind. Want me to go change?"

"Nah, you're good. I think I may feel a little safer being with you while you're still in your uniform," Chloe remarked as she reached over and flicked the collar of his shirt.

"Uniform or not, you're safe with me. Always. Mind, body and heart," he reminded her and gave her a sly wink. He hoped she read between the lines. He didn't want to start such a serious conversation at that moment, but he wanted her to know that he'd always treat her and her heart like a piece of fine china. There was no way he could treat her the way that Rico did. He hated to compare himself to her husband, but she needed to know that he was different.

"What?" Chloe exclaimed when she noticed that they were pulling up to Elliston Place Soda Shop. "I haven't been here in forever. I can't believe they're still around!"

Elliston Place Soda Shop was one of the oldest Nashville restaurants around. Chloe and Shane visited often during their high-school years. They spent a lot of time in that place, especially during senior year—her drinking a dreamsicle milkshake and him having a root beer float. They'd shared many stories about friends and love interests over their milkshakes. Just seeing the place brought back so many memories. In fact, they were here the first time he admitted that he was developing romantic feelings for her. She smiled at the thought and wondered if he remembered.

"I'm pretty cool, right?" he asked as he slid out of his seat and came around to open her door.

"You might be after this. If the milkshakes are still good, then I'll give you points for choosing this spot." He extended his arm and she looped her arm in his as they walked into the shop.

Not much had changed since she'd last been inside. The juke boxes, barstools, and black and white tiled walls took her mind back nearly twenty years. The juke box even played a popular song from their high school days as they walked inside. She inhaled, taking in the smell of fries and burgers. It felt just like home.

She noticed the restaurant had plaques on the walls with names of long-time customers. Shane walked her over to a booth not far from the entrance and gestured for her to have a seat. She glanced at the plaque above their seating area and noticed that it read, "Thank you for your patronage over the years—Shane McDaniels, long-time customer."

She pointed to the plaque. "Really Shane?" She then burst into laughter. "You brought me all the way here just so that I could see that your name was on the wall? Aren't we prideful? Tsk. Tsk." Chloe continued to tease.

He joined her in laughter. "Of course not, but it is pretty cool, right?" he asked. She nodded and the waitress came over and took their milkshake orders.

"This brings back a lot of memories, right?" Shane asked, echoing the thoughts she had when they first arrived. He reached across the table and rubbed her hands for a brief moment. He didn't linger too long, just enough to share a moment with her. He didn't want to make her feel uncomfortable, because he still wasn't quite certain where he stood with her or what was going on with her and Rico. She had yet to tell Shane that she was officially divorcing Rico.

"It does bring back memories. Many talks between us, huh? Secrets. Deep, dark, secrets," she whispered.

"You're so silly," he said and laughed. "So how are things at the hospital? Still adjusting well? Are they treating you right over there?"

"Yeah, it's good. Very good. In fact, I'm staying," she answered and allowed her statement to sink in.

Shane's eyes widened.

"What do you mean staying? In Nashville? For good?" He tried his best to hide his excitement.

"Yep," she answered and nodded simultaneously, watching him closely. She saw the question in his eyes and told him about her impending divorce. She was done. There was no way that she could stay in a marriage where there was no trust. She didn't think she'd be able to recover from that or get over what he did to her. It would always haunt her and she didn't want to live her life that way. No relationship was worth her sanity.

The waitress returned with their milkshakes, giving Shane a moment to digest what he'd just heard. Chloe was leaving her husband. Although that is what he wanted to happen, he knew that it hurt Chloe to give up that part of her life. He'd never been married, but he could only imagine how she must be feeling. He could only hope that this meant that he would finally get a chance to show her how much he loved her, but that would have to be some time in the future. How hard did he have to work to prove his love to her? How long would it take her to give him an opportunity to show her? That remained to be seen.

"Do you still love him?" Shane wondered aloud. He braced himself for what her answer might be as he took a sip of his milkshake. In fact, he knew the answer already, but he wanted to hear it from her. There was no way she didn't love him. If she didn't, this would be easier for her, but he could see the pain in her eyes. She was starting over and that had to be hard.

"Yes, but I don't love him enough to stay," she said, and took a sip of her milkshake before continuing. "Love isn't enough anymore," she told him. "I really tried to get past the infidelity. In fact, I stayed with him far longer than I should have trying to work things out by going to counseling sessions, among other things, but the pain is just too much to bear. I know the Bible says that God doesn't give us more than we can bear, but I feel like the weight of this thing is too much. It's like I'm in a boxing ring, unable to recover from a punch to the gut. I have to tap out."

"You're a good woman, Chloe. God will give you the strength you need," Shane encouraged. He got up from his seat, slid into the booth next to her and slipped his arms around her shoulders, squeezing her tightly. This wasn't exactly what he had in mind for their date, but it was definitely needed, given their circumstances. Part of him felt like this could be his opportunity, but the greater part of him knew that she just needed a friend. Someone she could lean on. And of course he would make himself available.

CHAPTER 25

Chloe talked Kelly into accompanying her back to Houston to pick up some of her things for her new place. She really liked a few decorative items that she purchased for the home she once shared with Rico, and she wanted them for her new home. Kelly agreed to tag along, leaving her children with their grandparents, hoping that the long ride would provide yet another opportunity for her to help Chloe sort through her thoughts, if she needed to, after what they'd recently learned about their mom.

The drive to Houston was far from the way Kelly imagined it would be. Kelly hadn't realized that Chloe had completely made up her mind about the situation. Nothing about their parents' situation seemed to have an effect on Chloe's decision. Chloe talked about how she'd been studying her Bible and the Texas state law and had come to terms with the fact that she had the biblical and legal right to divorce Rico because of his unfaithfulness. That gave her peace when it came to her relationship with God, but still left a hole in her heart. She'd spent the last decade of her life in a relationship with this man, and this is how it was going to end. What she needed God to fix was the hate that was building up in her heart for Rico, because she was certain the Bible only encouraged her to love and not hate.

Chloe was relieved that Rico's car wasn't parked in the driveway when she pulled up to their home. She wasn't planning to stay long, only long enough to grab her things, and she and her sister would crash in a hotel for a few days to allow her to tie up loose ends at her old job and make sure she had everything she wanted before saying good-bye to Rico and Houston forever. This was it for her.

The familiar scent of lavender kissed her nostrils as she entered the front door. Nothing had changed. Everything was just as she remembered. Even the vacuum cleaner was in the same place. She walked around the living room, with Kelly trailing slowly and silently behind her. She ran her hands along the leather reclining sofa that she'd purchased months before leaving. She loved that sofa and wished that she could take it with her, but there was no way it would fit in her coupe. She could hire movers but it didn't mean that much to her. She actually wanted as few memories of her relationship with Rico as possible in her new abode.

Kelly watched her sister as she seemed to walk around in a daze, maybe reminiscing about what used to be. Kelly despised Rico for what he'd done to Chloe, but tried to keep her opinion about him to herself as much as possible. Her sister didn't need the extra headache. Besides, if Chloe ever decided to get back with him, she'd likely be reluctant to share anything with her for a while knowing how she actually felt about him. Chloe had to make her decisions on her own, good or bad, whether or not Kelly agreed with them. After all, it was Chloe's life. Who knows whether she would come to regret her decision?

Chloe picked up a photo of herself and Kelly, taken at her wedding reception.

"Kel, remember this?" Chloe asked and smiled. Kelly walked over and looked at the photo of the two of them with goofy smiles on their faces. The happiness could be seen in their eyes. Their arms were wrapped around each other's waists while holding up the peace sign with the other hand. She grinned, recalling the moment that picture was taken. The sisters had just finished pulling off one of their routines that they had performed on their high school's dance team. That was a favorite of everyone who had any knowledge of their dance team. Kelly encouraged Chloe to do it with her. Chloe was reluctant at first, but the moment the DJ spun Michael Jackson's "PYT" at Kelly's request, Chloe couldn't resist.

"Yeah honey, that was so much fun! I'm glad you weren't such a stick in the mud and got out on that dance floor with me. I think everyone would agree that you worked it in your wedding dress," Kelly commented, nudging her sister with her shoulders. Kelly became serious and asked, "Do you ever stop to think about why you married Rico in the first place? Or how you felt on your wedding night?"

"All the time," Chloe answered as she placed the photo back on the table. She closed her eyes and took a deep breath. "And I wonder how we ever got to this place, you know? But don't think I don't know what you're trying to do here; it's not gonna work," Chloe wagged her finger at Kelly to prevent her from going down memory lane. She didn't want to think of that. She'd been doing that throughout this fiasco and it didn't get her anywhere. There was no need for any of that now.

"What?" Kelly asked, surprised. "I'm not doing anything. I just want to know how you're feeling . . . trying to make sure you're really okay with all of this, you know?"

Chloe simply nodded and continued to collect what she came back to the house to get. They walked around the house as Chloe took a painting, sconce or décor item here and there. She had purchased most of the things from arts and craft shows. She couldn't find the special items anywhere else. Most of them, Rico didn't care for anyway, so she was certain he wouldn't mind.

Chloe started up the stairs to their bedroom but changed her mind midway. She couldn't go in there again, not even if she wanted to. The thought of being in there reminded her of Rico being with Raegan; whether or not he'd been in there with her, she couldn't help but imagine that it happened. That same thought haunted her the moment she'd found out about the affair.

"What's wrong?" Kelly asked when she noticed Chloe's hesitation.

"Nothing. I'm going to go in the kitchen and grab my china. Will you get the rest of my clothes and pack them in the luggage that's left? Everything that you need is in my closet."

Kelly recognized the pained look on her face and didn't ask any questions; instead she did what she was asked to do. Chloe rummaged through the curio cabinet and began wrapping her dishes and the glass slipper, made of real glass, she purchased from a diamond shop at Magic Kingdom in Disney World. That was a happy time in their lives, and if she wanted to hold any memory of him at all, it may as well be a happy one. Besides, Rico couldn't have cared less about things like that.

She nearly dropped the glass slipper when she felt Rico's hand on her shoulder. Why would he walk up to her without saying a word?

"Hey," was all he managed to say. He thought he was hallucinating when he pulled into the driveway and saw her car and smelled her perfume when he entered the door. He was too afraid to say anything for fear she might disappear. But he wasn't imagining things. Chloe was back. Hopefully he could convince her to stay.

Chloe whispered "hello" and looked down at his hand touching her shoulder until he dropped it. It appeared to be a little frail, so she assumed that he hadn't been eating as well as he should and was under a lot of stress because of how things were unfolding between them. She tilted her head up so that her eyes could meet his, and she noticed that he didn't look well. He looked as if he hadn't had much sleep and was possibly battling a bad cold.

Rico wanted to scoop her into his arms and kiss her, but he knew she wouldn't have that. Instead they both stood there. Silent. Chloe was waiting for him to move out of her way while Rico was trying to think of another way to ask her to stay. Kelly stood behind him at the foot of the stairs watching the interaction. Time stood still and everyone was silent waiting for someone else to make the next move.

"I'll come back later," Chloe finally said, choking back tears. Him standing there in front of her like that, everything in his eyes begging her to stay, was just too much for her to handle. She didn't think she'd be emotional if she were to run into Rico, yet there she was about to burst into tears. She thought she'd tucked away whatever feelings she had left for him, but her heart made it known that she hadn't. She slid past him, dabbing at her eyes, hurriedly walking toward the front door, with Kelly on her heels carrying the suitcase she'd lugged from upstairs.

And she vanished, just as Rico was afraid she would.

CHAPTER 26

Chloe's mind was preoccupied with the disappointed look painted on Rico's face yesterday as she turned to walk out the door. She'd hoped he didn't think she was there to stay. After long moments of silence, he finally stepped to the side to allow her to pass, if she so chose. And she did. Although her heart reached out to him, she couldn't will herself to stay. Not anymore. Her mind was made up.

This was day two of wrapping things up, and all she needed to do was return to the hospital and fill out some exit paperwork since she'd accepted a full-time position back in Nashville. There was nothing left for her in Houston.

The aroma of disinfectant filled her nostrils as she walked the place where she'd spent the last several years of her career. The scent bothered many people, but she kind of liked it. It reminded her of home; in fact, this was her home. Caught up in her feelings, she halfway didn't recognize the woman who bumped into her as she exited one of the patient rooms.

"Excuse you!" the woman said with a nasty attitude.

Chloe turned around trying to get a good look at the woman. Her voice reminded her of her soon-to-be-ex-sister-in-law Diane. Chloe shuddered at the thought. That woman always had it in for her. Diane in her life was definitely something she wouldn't miss.

The woman didn't turn around and Chloe didn't bother to address her. *No way that could have been her,* Chloe thought. She was one step closer to leaving Houston for good and starting her new life; no one was going to interfere with that.

Chloe continued walking to the nurses' station to visit some of her colleagues before getting to what she came to do.

Both Sherrie and Karen looked up from their tablets and gave half-smiles before expressing their prayer offerings to her regarding Rico's condition.

"We're so sorry dear; we'll be praying for your family. The doctors have been doing all they can do for him," Karen told her.

Chloe took a step back and glanced down the hall. Diane was really there with all of her rudeness. And Rico? What was going on with him? Why didn't he say anything? What were the nurses talking about? She didn't want to ask because she didn't want them in her business. She wanted to be upset with them for bringing it up, but there was no way, to her knowledge, they would know that she and Rico were done. Apparently they were being sincere.

"Thank you," Chloe said slowly as she turned to look for Diane again.

"Oh, I'll take you to his room," Karen offered, jumping up out of her seat, assuming that was the reason for Chloe's visit.

Chloe hesitantly followed Karen about fifty feet away from the nurses' station, not knowing what would be behind that patient door. She braced herself for the worst as Karen opened the door for her. Chloe stepped to the side as Karen closed the door behind her and then walked over to Rico's side, grazing his hand with hers to wake him. The cool air caused chill bumps to cover her arms. She'd entered in and out of patient rooms many times and the temperature never seemed to bother her; but today was different. She seemed to feel every degree.

Rico was hooked up to all sorts of machines as he lay in the hospital bed. His face looked pale and his hands felt cold. He looked nothing like the man she left a few months ago. She could tell that something was wrong when she saw him a couple of days ago, but she just assumed that maybe he had a bad cold and wasn't taking care of himself like he should. Never anything like this.

Rico batted his eyes weakly before opening them to see Chloe standing at his side.

"What are you doing here? Who told you?" His voice was strained and his throat seemed dry. Chloe handed him a cup of water that was sitting on the table next to his bed. She waited for him to take a sip before responding to his questions.

"I don't know much of anything. I'm hoping you can tell me . . . what's going on with you? What is all of this? Why didn't you say anything?"

"I didn't want you coming back to me out of pity; I wanted you to come back because you love me and you're willing to forgive me. And be with me until it's all over."

Over. When Chloe wanted things to be over between her and Rico, this was not what she had in mind. She quickly blinked back the tears that were threatening to erupt. She needed to find out exactly what was going on.

"What do you mean?" she questioned, her voice barely above a whisper.

"I have stage four prostate cancer. I am going through chemo in hopes that God would turn this thing around for me, but the doctors say it's too late and it's not working. But I am holding on to hope that God will give me a different report."

Chloe pulled the chair closer to the bed and took a seat. She'd known patients as young as Rico to beat prostate cancer; it broke her heart to know that the odds weren't in his favor. She grabbed Rico's hand and held it for what seemed like eternity. That was the same hand that held hers when he asked for her hand in marriage. The same hand the pastor placed hers in when he pronounced them man and wife. The same hand that grabbed hers when he begged her forgiveness after his affair with Raegan. Now that hand would no longer be there for her to hold.

"I don't believe it; I want to talk to the doctors," Chloe demanded.

"No," Rico stated firmly and gripped her hand as tight as he could with the little strength that he had left. "Don't." He shook his head lightly and winced.

Chloe looked over at him and he shook his head as if to say that her efforts would be futile. He looked defeated. He was no longer the confident, often arrogant, man she once knew. His eyes were tired and his face almost looked as if he were wearing a frown. But she knew better; he was just weak from the chemo.

"You know, I started getting my life together. Prayer. Church. Ministry groups. More prayer. Reading my Bible. More church. When I first started, I have to admit that I was doing all of that to get you back, but then I realized that something important in my life was missing. Always had been. An honest and true relationship with God. I believe that if I had that in the beginning, I would have known how to treat you and I never would have done all of the things I did. I know it won't happen overnight, but I hope you'll find it in your heart to truly forgive me someday. I don't think I can ever express how sorry I am for not honoring you as the wife the Lord gave to me. The Bible says to love your wife as yourself, and if I had loved you even more than I loved myself, shoot, even half of the amount I love myself, I would have treated you better. But now I know the error of my ways and have truly sought the Lord's forgiveness. I know He has forgiven me, but I'd surely rest better knowing you forgive me too. I'm sorry," Rico's voice cracked at the end of his speech.

Chloe smiled through the tears streaming down her face. That was the most sincere apology that she'd received from Rico regarding his indiscretions. And who knows? If his apology had been that sincere early on, she may have taken him back. But it was too late to think about that now. She placed both hands around his and kissed them.

"God bless you for your growth and strength. Even if it is at this point, I'm happy I got a chance to witness it," Chloe said after swallowing the lump in her throat, intentionally avoiding the subject of forgiveness.

"I know I haven't shown it much over the last couple of years but I love you. Never forget that," Rico said.

Interrupting their moment, Diane burst through the door, loud and uncouth as usual.

"Oh *now* she wants to show up?" Diane snarled.

Chloe's frame tensed up at Diane's outburst. Refusing to be on the receiving end of Diane's shenanigans, Chloe dropped Rico's hand and walked over to confront her. She was always in their business thinking that she knew what was right, wrong or impossible. But she picked the wrong person on the wrong day. Chloe had had enough of her and it was time Diane knew it.

CHAPTER 27

"Hmph!" Diane grunted and inched toward Chloe, who stood in the center of the room with her arms folded.

"You know what? I've had just about enough of your foolishness to last me a lifetime. Don't you see your brother is lying up in this hospital bed sick?" Chloe turned to point at Rico, who seemed to be panicking as he searched around his bed for the call button. "Why are you coming in here starting mess? Today of all days?"

"Whatever!" Diane pointed a finger in Chloe's face. "Why are you even here now? Where were you when he needed you the most? When he first found out he had cancer? A poor excuse for a wife – that's what you are!"

Chloe's heart skipped a beat at the mention of Rico's cancer, but continued to argue with Diane. In a normal situation, she would be trying to deal with the fact that her husband was possibly dying, but this wasn't an ordinary situation and Diane wasn't a normal person. She had to deal with her in this moment or Diane would keep acting as if she'd lost her mind.

"Now you wait one minute!" Chloe interrupted Diane's speech, but Diane ignored her and continued.

"No one in this room needs you. Why don't you just go back to whatever rock you crawled from up under? Stuck-up tramp!" She'd been waiting on a moment where she could tell Chloe how she really felt about her. Now that her brother and Chloe's relationship was about over, this was the perfect opportunity.

"Why are you forty years old still name-calling? You need to get a life and stay out of mine. All you've ever done is stir up mess and frankly I'm tired of your crap! If you don't get your finger out of my face, I will rip it off!" Chloe threatened through clenched teeth, stepping closer to Diane, daring her to keep up her childish antics.

"Doesn't the Bible tell you to turn the other cheek? I thought you were a Christian! Figures you are fake about that as well," Diane continued slinging insults, meeting Chloe's dare.

"My Christianity is not in question. But don't play me. I've had enough of you, so I'm seconds away from putting you in a hospital bed. Luckily you don't have far to go." Chloe eyed Diane, daring her to make a move. Fighting anyone was not in her character, but she'd been waiting just as long as Diane to be honest about her disgust for her. After all, Diane always made it clear that she despised her and would have rather had anyone else for a sister-in-law.

Rico pressed the button on the remote to alert his nurse to come into the room. He was weak and ordinarily he would have shushed Diane before she went too far, but he was in no position to do that today.

"Is everything all right?" nurse Karen asked, rushing into the room. She noted that from the looks on their faces, there was about to be a showdown between Diane and Chloe.

"Yeah," Chloe said curtly, stepping away and returning to her seat at Rico's side. Rico never really stood up to Diane for the way she treated Chloe. That was another issue that she had with him. She knew that was his sister, but he never put his foot down to remind her that they were one and if nothing else, had to treat her and their marriage with respect.

Nurse Karen eyed each of them carefully. The tension in the atmosphere was unmistakable, especially with the scowl covering Diane's face as she remained planted in the center of the room where she and Chloe had their confrontation.

"The patient should probably be getting some rest. How about you two take a break?" she said to Chloe and Diane, and reminded them of the cafeteria downstairs.

Diane grabbed her purse and shot Chloe a look that said *this isn't over*. She stormed out of the room as Chloe remained seated. She wasn't one to overstep authority, but she had unfinished business with Rico. Rico nodded to the nurse, letting her know that he was fine and Chloe could stay. Seeing that her patient was comfortable, she left the two of them alone.

Through weak and raspy breaths, Rico apologized for Diane's behavior, as he'd always done. But that was opposite of what Chloe wanted. She'd wanted him to stand up for her, for their marriage, and tell his sister to stay out of their business. It seemed as if he was yet making another excuse for Diane and she didn't want to hear it. She held up her hand to stop him. Memories of their relationship flashed through her mind as she sat holding Rico's hand. "Are you going to stay?" Rico asked, his weak voice hopeful.

Chloe nodded. The moment she saw him lying in that hospital bed, the feelings of anger and resentment she'd been harboring toward him for ruining their marriage were replaced with compassion. Her job in Nashville would have to wait. Her moving. Her resignation. Everything would have to be put on hold. Their divorce wasn't final, so she would keep her vows. She would be there for him even though he hadn't been there for her. As much as she wanted to hold that against him, she couldn't leave him at a time like this. What kind of kind of wife would she be?

"Will you forgive me?" he asked directly this time.

Now that was something she didn't have an answer to. Did she love him? Yes. Would she keep her vows? Yes. But she wasn't ready to forgive him yet. She couldn't; it still hurt too badly. The betrayal. The intentional disregard for her as his wife. The web of lies.

"One step at a time," she answered. The chemo was wearing on him and he was starting to nod off to sleep. Chloe gave his hand a tight squeeze, told him she'd be back, grabbed her things and headed for her car. Her initial reason for coming to the hospital was far from her mind. No paperwork today. She would call and get things straightened out with her boss later.

Is this God's way of making me stay with my husband? she wondered as she walked mindlessly through the hospital, steps she'd taken thousands of times, but none ever felt like this. There was a chance that her marriage to Rico was really about to be over, and not because of the divorce but because *death was about to part them.* Even though she wanted out of her marriage before, this was different. She didn't want it to end like this, so she prayed for Rico. She'd prayed for him daily up until she found out about his last affair. The old Bible verse of *praying for your enemies* had become tough. But now, he wasn't an enemy, he was just her husband in need of God's healing.

If God healed him, would she call off the divorce? She wasn't certain, but she was sure that she wouldn't want Rico's life to end this way. When she made it to her car, she sat there for quite a while crying and thinking about every moment that led up to this point. Was this how it was destined to end for them?

Gathering the strength to withhold her tears, she started the car and headed for the hotel. How was she even supposed to handle all of this?

CHAPTER 28

When Chloe arrived back at the hotel room she and Kelly were sharing, she kicked off her shoes and plopped down across the queen-sized bed. Without a word to Kelly, she buried her face in the comforter, laughing and crying hysterically while her sister sat in the other queen-sized bed reading a magazine that she'd picked up in a convenience store earlier that day.

"Paperwork was that bad, huh?" Kelly commented, putting her magazine aside and sliding to the edge of her bed. She sat perched at the end of the bed waiting for her sister's response, which was taking a moment too long, in her opinion. When Chloe's antics ceased and she didn't move from the spot she occupied, Kelly clicked off the TV that was airing an old nineties movie and moved to her sister's bed.

"Rico." Chloe's one word was muffled but clear.

"Ummm, you're gonna have to give me more than that. You haven't mentioned him since we saw him at the house. Was he waiting for you at the hospital?"

Chloe shook her head and buried her face into the comforter once more as if that would help her feel any better. Kelly rubbed Chloe's back and waited for her to lift her head and tell her what happened.

"Cancer. Can you believe that?"

"Rico?" Kelly asked, seemingly confused.

Chloe nodded and shared how she found out about Rico's prostate cancer and her run-in with Diane while at the hospital. Chloe's eyes were swollen and red from crying. Her lips trembled as she recalled the events. She went from compassionate about Rico to angry about his sister Diane.

"I'm going to ask that they postpone my official start date back home. I can't leave him like this. Through sickness and health, right?" Chloe solemnly asked, holding up her hand to finger the shadow on her finger that once housed her wedding band.

"Oh, I'm sorry sis!" Kelly said and gasped, pulling her sister in her arms for a tight squeeze. Chloe's arms dangled at her side, allowing herself the comfort of her sister's hug. This wasn't the way Kelly would have wanted God to work things out, but hopefully He had heard her prayers and this situation would somehow turn out for Chloe's good and bring her the peace that she was desperately seeking.

"Wait . . . if you're here with your husband, what does this mean for that little thing you had going on at home with Shane?" Kelly asked. Now probably wasn't the best time to bring up the thing she and Shane had going on, but it needed to be addressed. *Shane,* Chloe thought to herself. She hadn't spoken to him since she arrived in Houston. He'd called and texted her several times today, but she had yet to respond. She was certain he was concerned and probably ready to put out an APB on her.

"I have no idea," answered Chloe. Chloe walked over to the window, rubbing the chills bumps on her arms, even though the thermostat read 78.

Chloe found herself upset with Rico for once again interrupting her life and changing her plans. The original plan was to be his wife until death parted them, and he ruined that. She had just settled with the idea that their marriage couldn't work. She was moving on with her life in a different city and she would see how things worked out with Shane when she was ready, after the divorce. Now all of that was being put on pause because she could not neglect her wifely duties. She wouldn't be any better than Rico if she left him while he was on his sickbed, potentially about to lose his life. She couldn't truly be happy and find peace if she knew he was suffering, and she was quite sure that he wouldn't be able to find peace knowing that she'd moved on and left him while he was down. No one deserved that, not even Rico, after all that he'd put her through.

"I want you to be happy, sis. I just think that you need to make sure that things are really over with you and your husband before you go staking a claim to Shane." Kelly patted the vacant seat next to her on the bed.

Chloe blew out a loud, hard sigh and shook her head. Instead of accepting Kelly's invitation to sit, she picked up her cell phone, slid back into her shoes and walked out of the room. Her head was hurting enough trying to process everything that was happening; she didn't need a lecture on how to manage her relationship with Shane or Rico. She needed to call Shane and explain things to him. She'd been honest with him from the start. He understood that she was still married and that came along with certain responsibilities until her divorce was final. She'd already voiced that she still loved Rico; Shane knew her well enough to know she wouldn't leave Rico hanging at a time like this.

CHAPTER 29

Rico sat propped up in his hospital bed, mouth dry, body in pain and feeling an overwhelming sense of fatigue. His mind drifted to thoughts of Raegan and how he'd hurt her. He had to make things right, but he was sure she wouldn't take any of his calls. And now that she was married, her husband would certainly not allow him to get anywhere near her. But he'd try anyway. He picked up the phone near his bed and pecked at the numbers etched in his memory. Holding the phone to his ear, he held his breath until he heard the line open.

Raegan's body stiffened at the sound of the weak voice on the other end of the call. The voice was faint but it made her skin crawl. No matter how pathetic the voice sounded, she would always have it ingrained in her mind. Rico. Whispering apologies. Before seeing him at the park several months ago, she hadn't talked to him since that day in the coffee shop when she had him sign over his parental rights. His voice reminded her of all the horrible things that happened in her life, and she didn't need those memories, so she disconnected the call.

Raegan hanging up on him confirmed that a part of her still held on to the heartache he caused her. Seeing as though Raegan would likely never accept a phone call from him again, Rico drafted an e-mail for her on his phone. He wrote in hopes that she would read it and accept his apology, so that he could have a clear conscience. He'd have to live with the realization that she would likely dismiss him, but he wasn't going to let that stop him from asking for forgiveness. Besides, he knew that she believed in the Word of God. *Forgive and be forgiven,* he thought. If nothing else, perhaps she would forgive him because God said so. He even added a few words to tell her about his cancer, hoping that would spark a warm spot in her heart and help her to forgive him, if she hadn't already. Hitting *send,* he breathed a sigh of relief. She had to know that it was never his intent to hurt her or wreak havoc in her life. Although it was wrong, he did have feelings for her and he wanted her to know that his feelings were always genuine. She was a beautiful woman—inside and out.

Raegan wanted to delete Rico's e-mail but felt compelled to open it since he hadn't reached out to her in some time. A large knot formed in her throat when she learned of his cancer. She'd despised him for messing over her life, but she never wished that level of harm to him. She and Caleb never talked about Rico since seeing him in the park, but she wanted her husband to read the e-mail as well. They both needed to forgive Rico. She was certain that Caleb held a level of disgust for him just as much as she did.

Raegan walked into the twins' room where Caleb was rocking one of them to sleep while the other sat on the floor rolling a ball with Nicholas. They were a beautiful sight. Raegan squatted on the floor, placed the other twin in her lap and began rolling the ball to Nicholas after handing her phone to Caleb so he could read the e-mail.

"Babe, we have all that we need now. All is forgiven. He can move on. We have," Caleb said, handing the phone back to her and kissing her lips. Caleb had realized that day in the park that he'd forgiven Rico, because he didn't smash his face in when he saw him. In fact, the moment Rico continued his run, Caleb didn't think about him anymore, nor did he mention him to his wife. Everything he wanted and needed was right in that room with him. Rico's lies had no gripping hold on his spirit, and he hoped the same was true for Raegan.

Raegan took the phone and responded to his e-mail, "We forgive you." There was no reason to write anything else or get into any back and forth correspondence. Although she felt a sense of compassion for him regarding his illness, she made no mention of it in her reply. She figured he was trying to clear his conscience and she would give him that. They had no ties and no reason to remain connected. She hoped that one day she would be able to hear his name and not cringe, but today wasn't it. However, she had to be grateful to him for one thing: If it wasn't for him, she probably would have never reconnected with the man she loved with all of her heart; so there was a rainbow after the storm. Hopefully, she would learn to associate his name with helping her get to where she needed to be—with Caleb—instead of the lies and false dreams that he sold to her. And with that, she smiled and turned her phone off, joining in playtime with her family. One thing was for sure, Caleb was right when he said they had all that they needed. She hoped that Rico could say the same.

Rico was relieved when he received a response from Raegan. *We?* He grinned at the response. He wouldn't have expected anything less. Now he could breathe. His concentration now was making sure that Chloe forgave him. There was nothing like a life and death situation that made people want to correct their wrongs. His wrongs with Chloe had to be made right.

∞

"How long will you be in Houston?" Shane asked. The disappointment was evident in his voice. He understood Chloe's loyalty to her cheating husband, but it didn't hurt any less that she was staying in Houston with him—no matter how long. He thought he was finally going to get his chance with her and prove to her that he could give her the kind of love she deserved.

Shane was greeted with silence as Chloe shrugged her shoulders in response to his question. Shane was starting to grow on her once again, so she hated to leave him out in the cold, but she was married. That was her reasoning for never wanting to get close to Shane in the first place. Each time it seemed as if their friendship was crossing the line, she'd reminded him that she was still legally married to Rico; their divorce was not yet final. He'd always seemed like he was okay with that, but the pain she heard through the telephone line told her much different.

She should have known better. There was no way that Shane would have ever been okay with her messy life. But it was too late for that now because he had been immersed in it.

"I'm not sure; as long as Rico needs me," Chloe finally responded in a hushed tone as she sat in her parked car, running her fingers along the steering wheel. This was difficult for her. She felt like she was breaking up with him and they weren't even together. It reminded her of the moment they shared many years ago when they had gotten close and she told him that they could only be friends.

Chloe cared for Shane but the facts were still the same. She was married to Rico and she would fulfill her vows. She had never committed to Shane in any way, so why should she feel bad? *Because I care for him,* her conscience reminded her.

"I see." The bouts of silence on the line were deafening, neither one wanting to say good-bye and end things again. But Shane knew there was always a possibility that Chloe would go back to Rico. She'd already admitted that she still loved him. "So no divorce?" Shane asked after another round of quietness. That was the important question. If there would be no divorce, there really wasn't any reason for him to wait around for her to come back.

"I didn't say that . . . it's just that Rico needs me and I'm still his wife. I can't leave him like this, Shane. You understand that, right?" Chloe's question sounded somewhat like a plea and an apology wrapped into one. She couldn't believe that she was about to cry over a man she wasn't married to. She paused to wonder if that is how Rico felt when he signed over his parental rights to Raegan's baby—he was giving up something he really wanted for the sake of making his marriage work. But she wasn't doing this to make her marriage work, only to honor the vows that she'd taken. And because of the growing feelings she had for Shane, she was now coming to regret them. "I'm sorry, Shane." She didn't know what else to say, she only knew that she had to do what was right. She pulled the phone away from her mouth to exhale and to keep herself from bawling.

"Me, too. See you later Chloe." Shane cleared his throat and agreed. Before ending the call, he held the phone and that bout of silence slapped him in the face again. He didn't know what he was waiting for, maybe for her to change her mind and say that she was on her way back to him or to say that when everything was well with Rico, she would give their relationship a chance. Or maybe even a profession of love? He wanted something to hold on to, some hope that she was definitely planning to come back to Nashville at some point so that they could pick up where they left off.

What am I doing? She's another man's wife, Shane inwardly chastised himself. He believed that you reap what you sow and he didn't want any issues in his marriage whenever the time came. He had to back off. If anything were to happen between him and Chloe, she would have to be the one to come to him. He had made it clear on several occasions that he had feelings for her. But since she was still married, there was nothing that could be done to explore either of their feelings. After ending the call, he decided that he had no choice but to let it go.

For now.

CHAPTER 30

Rico finished his chemo treatment. He'd been praying that God would move on his behalf and remove the cancer from his body. He didn't care what stage it was in. He'd been studying his Bible and reading about how God healed the sick and even brought people back from the dead. If God could do it for them, surely He could do it for him and for his marriage too. Chloe returned to the hospital to take Rico home. Kelly was a little disappointed that Chloe wasn't returning to Nashville with her, but understood Chloe's need to take care of Rico, so she accepted Chloe's offer to buy her a plane ticket back home. She needed to get back to her children anyway.

"You all set?" Chloe asked Rico as she entered his room. The atmosphere was so much different with Diane gone home. She was glad that Rico had the support of family before she was aware of his cancer, but relieved that Diane didn't stay this time. She wasn't sure how often Diane had been in Houston since she left for Nashville; she was just grateful that she wasn't there now.

Rico was dressed, sitting in his bed, flipping channels. His face glowed when he saw her. She hadn't seen that look since early in their marriage. That was the Rico she knew. Although things were pretty bad between them, she welcomed the warmth.

"Yes ma'am." He clicked off the TV and moved to stand. His nurse came through the door with a wheelchair the moment he hopped to his feet. She admonished him for trying to move too fast and suggested that he take it easy and ride to the car instead of walking. Taking orders, he took a seat and waited for the nurse to escort them down to the car.

"I don't mind pushing," Chloe said to the nurse, taking over behind the chair. Rico covered one of her hands with his on the journey to the car. She did nothing to remove his hand. In fact, she welcomed the gesture, but just wished that their circumstances were different. Why did it take him being sick to appreciate her?

When they arrived downstairs, the nurse helped Rico out of the wheelchair and charged him to take it easy until she saw him again in a few weeks.

"You got it!" Rico said. He'd been praying for healing and would do whatever was asked of him in hopes that God would see his sincerity and grant his request. His newfound obedience had to count for something, in his opinion. It was downright backward theology and he knew that he couldn't bargain with God, but he was desperate and would do anything for restored health.

"Thank you," Rico began when Chloe started the car. When she removed her hand from the keys he engulfed it in his. "I mean it. You didn't have to do any of this. You could have packed your things and left me here. I deserve that after the way I treated you. And believe me, if there was a way that I could take it all back, I would. So thank you for being a better partner in this marriage than I have been." He lifted her hand to his lips and caressed it with the most gentle kiss he'd ever given her.

"You're welcome." Chloe slid her hand out of his, shifted the car into gear and pulled out of the waiting area. She spent the next several seconds fighting to hold back the tears that were threatening to escape from her eyes. That was the second heartfelt apology he'd given her. *Where was this man a couple of years ago?* She wondered.

The ride back to their home was mostly silent with the exception of small talk about the weather, work and the Texans' winning streak. They avoided the topic of their impending divorce. Rico wondered if she planned to withdraw her petition; he'd hoped that she had a change of heart. Even if she didn't, he planned to spend the time they had together getting her to change her mind about them. Now that she was back, no matter how temporarily, she could see that he was really a changed man, and he owed it all to God.

Chloe grinned ruefully when she pulled up to their house. When she drove here a few days ago, that was supposed to be her last time laying eyes on that house. Now, not only was she coming back, she was there with the man she never wanted to see again, or at least that's how she felt a few days ago.

She hopped out of the car and went around to the passenger side to help Rico out of the car and into the house. She wrapped her arm around his waist and he followed suit as they walked the path to the front door. Rico loved every second of that and intentionally took smaller steps to drag out the moment, while Chloe didn't know how to feel about it. She would have to admit that on one level it was nice being close to her husband like that again. That was the most intimate moment she'd experienced with him since finding out about his affair with Raegan. She'd refused to let him get within two feet of her after finding out he betrayed their marriage and her trust again.

"Are you hungry? I can go out to get groceries and make you something to eat," Chloe said as she helped him get situated on the couch.

"Perhaps I should have become a patient of yours a couple of years ago if this is the kind of treatment I'm going to get," Rico teased. Chloe laughed and that was a relief for him. The awkwardness was starting to slip away. Except for the closeness they'd just shared walking in the house, one would think they were strangers.

Chloe picked up a couch pillow and tagged him with it. She was glad that he still had his sense of humor and was refusing to let his disease get him down. Positive attitudes did wonders for most of her patients. She moved around and sat next to his feet that were now propped up on the couch.

"All that matters is that you're a patient now. So what do you say? I'm willing to cook whatever you want today. Don't try to take advantage of me though," she said and wagged her finger at him.

"I'll let you decide what we eat," he answered. He was just happy to have her back inside of their home. Her wanting to do things for him was a bonus. He'd take bread and water as long as she was serving it.

"Baked chicken it is!" she announced and moved to stand. She felt Rico tugging at her left hand, fingering the area that used to house her wedding band.

"This means a lot to me." The fact that she was sticking with him through all of this gave him hope that she would one day wear it again. There was so much more that he wanted to say. To tell her that he never stopped loving her. To apologize again for his infidelity and how it ruined their marriage. To tell her that if he could start over, he would make different choices. But he would save that for another time. For now, he would just give praise to his heavenly Father for the fact that she was there with him.

CHAPTER 31

Rico was on pins and needles not knowing where Chloe's mind was regarding their impending divorce, especially since she hadn't mentioned the papers. She'd been back for more than a week. She made sure he had his daily meals and medicine and took care of the cleaning around the house as if it was something she'd been doing the last few months. But it wasn't. She had been away, planning to never come back to him again.

Not knowing whether she was going to leave or go, coupled with the idea that he'd been stuck in the house for the last week, was driving Rico crazy. He needed to get out of the house before he lost his mind. The one thing that would keep him sane would be knowing that she had changed her mind about leaving him, but he put off asking her about it for fear that she would tell him that she would leave after he got better. Hearing that would surely send him straight to his final resting place.

"Let's get out of here. I feel like the walls are closing in on me," Rico complained, throwing his head back against the couch so that Chloe could hear him from the other room. His voice was still weak, as if he was fighting a terrible cold, but Chloe was in the next room and would easily be able to hear him. She'd been listening out for him in case he needed her. He sat propped up on the couch, just as he had been most of the week. His body was starting to hurt from sitting and sleeping in that same spot. They had two spare bedrooms, but there weren't any TVs in those rooms so he opted to stay on the sofa.

Chloe sauntered out of the kitchen at the sound of his whine, with one hand on her hip and a large cooking spoon in the other. She wagged the spoon and shook her head. She had gone over the rules for him nearly every day that week. He needed to be away from other people since he was taking chemo treatments, which made his immune system low. She refused to allow him to go anywhere that would compromise his health. She wasn't taking any risks, no matter how much he complained about being cooped up in the house. Better cooped up in the house than in a casket.

"We're just gonna have to do something fun around here. I'll open the window up a little more. But that's it. I'll let you know when we can go somewhere. Problem with that? Would you like to request another caretaker, mister?" Chloe turned around to ask after spreading the chocolate curtain panels and opening both windows in the living room and the nearest window in the kitchen to allow fresh air to flow through the house. As she'd done so, a wave of crisp, fresh air and rays of sunlight cut through the rooms. She paused for a moment, reveling in the breeze that entered the house. Even she was refreshed by the kiss from nature; she'd been in and out of the house a few times but for the most part had been in the house with Rico.

Rico shook his head and smiled. That was the Chloe he knew—taking charge and putting him in his place. He was starting to feel like she cared about him again.

Chloe walked back into the kitchen to check on her meal preparations. As she cut up potatoes to boil and mash, she thought of things that Rico liked that would cheer him up and get his mind off sitting around the house all day. After she finished chopping potatoes, she walked back into the living room, picked up the remote and switched the TV to video mode. It was time to dance! She switched on the Nintendo Wii, put in the Michael Jackson dance game and tossed a control stick to Rico.

"This is your something to do. I will not take it easy on you either," she teased, grabbing her own control stick and setting the game up for her favorite song: "Beat It."

Chloe stayed true to her word. The moment the beat dropped, she got into dance mode as if she were part of Michael

Jackson's dance team or MJ himself. He'd never recalled her playing the video game very much in the past, so he wondered how she'd learned all of the dance moves. He lost the first round because he was stunned to see her moving the way she did.

When the first song ended, she changed the song to "Smooth Criminal." This time Rico got into dance mode and allowed himself to have fun being silly with her, dancing as much as his body would allow, and often trying to get in the way of the monitor stick so that it wouldn't pick up her movements. She was kicking his butt. But they were having fun. They'd gone through song after song and she continued to dance the evening away, completely forgetting that she hadn't finished dinner.

After an hour and a half of non-stop dancing, her shirt was soaked with sweat and their faces were glowing from the fun they were having. Rico bent over, grabbing his knees and breathing heavily as if he'd just run a race. He'd done as much dancing as his body would allow, taking frequent breaks to watch her. Even though he was tired and out of breath during the songs he actually danced to, he continued on so that he could enjoy the moment with her. He couldn't remember the last time he'd enjoyed her company this way.

"Whew! That was a little intense. I think I needed that workout. I let you beat me though. I couldn't have you walking around here all sad because I won, so I let you have it. I'm not a sore loser." He held up his hand to high-five her but she left him hanging and walked away.

"Sounds like a sore loser to me," she tossed over her shoulder laughing, as she headed for the shower before she finished preparing dinner. All she'd done was cut the potatoes and place them in a pot of cold water. She enjoyed that time with Rico as much as he did. This was the first time she didn't think about his infidelity or wonder if he'd done the same thing with Raegan. Maybe this time together was what she needed; it could be the beginning of her being able leave their past behind them.

∞

"Smells good in here," Rico commented as he walked to the kitchen table and took a seat. Chloe scooped mashed potatoes and steamed vegetables onto their plates and added baked chicken breasts. She poured glasses of water and joined him at the table with their plates.

Rico reached for her hand to bless the food. Chloe hesitated and Rico could tell that she was surprised by his willingness to pray, as it hadn't been something that he did much of in the past. She was always the one to initiate prayer during dinner or any other time. After praying, he held firm to her hand, never wanting to let her go again.

"Chloe, I really am a different man than the one you left standing in the driveway a few months ago. God is the center of my life now, like He should have been from the beginning. And I promise if you give me another chance I can show you how things will be different," Rico pleaded.

There. He'd opened the door for discussion. He didn't know why he felt compelled to say something about their relationship at this moment, but it seemed like as good a time as any. Someone had to say something about where their relationship stood, and he figured he would be the one to do it since he was the one who messed it up. More than anything, he wanted her back in his life and he would spend every day he had left on the earth showing it to her, if she would give him the chance.

Chloe chewed her food thoughtfully as she contemplated Rico's plea. She hadn't said anything about the divorce for a reason. She didn't know whether or not she wanted to go through with it anymore. She was still working on getting past his infidelity, but lately that hadn't been an issue for her. Her focus had been making sure he got well and praying him through his chemo treatments. But now the issue was back on the table and they both needed to deal with their real feelings and whether or not they could make their marriage work—or if they were even willing. Could she submit to him as the Bible says she should? Could she still respect him as her husband? Follow his leadership? She couldn't answer those questions for herself, so wasn't sure if withdrawing her petition for divorce was the best thing for them just yet.

CHAPTER 32

"It's been a whole month! Does that mean I'm only going to see you during the holidays?" Kelly asked. She had gotten used to the idea that her sister would only be about a twenty-minute drive away. Kelly would support Chloe in whatever decision she made; she just wanted her to be at peace with it. She'd been praying for Chloe's strength and for God's will to be done in the situation ever since Chloe showed up on her doorstep.

"I don't know about all of that just yet," Chloe answered, lodging the phone between her ear and shoulder while she folded laundry.

She hadn't made up her mind about what she wanted to do, so she wasn't quite in the mood to talk about it or get Rico's hopes up and let Shane's hopes down. Rico was sitting in the next room watching TV, but she was sure his ears would perk up if there was any mention of her not moving to Nashville permanently as planned.

"Just promise me that you'll make the best decision for you and your marriage. Pray first, okay?"

"Promise . . . things have just been so crazy," Chloe said. It almost seemed as if she'd been given another chance to make a different decision. But as of now, she hadn't made a choice, so she would just keep on living and doing what she was supposed to do—keep her vows.

∞

Chloe reached for the car door handle but paused when she noticed Rico didn't make a move to get out of the car. When they pulled into the hospital's parking garage and found a parking space, Rico clasped his hands together and bowed his head. He felt the need to pray again before going inside. He needed to hear something different than what he'd heard when he was first diagnosed. From the beginning, the doctor warned him that his cancer was advanced and the chemo might not work, but his faith in God had nearly quadrupled. He had been praying that God would heal him and that maybe he would have a testimony like he used to hear about when he was growing up in church, but if He didn't, Rico had decided that he was okay with that. If his condition didn't do anything else, it helped push him to pray and study his Bible more. And for that, he was thankful because he'd gotten a chance to know God a little better, far better than he probably would have had this cancer or his failed marriage not happened.

Without lifting his head or opening his eyes, he reached for his wife's hand and held on as if it would be the last time. His grip was nearly painful but she didn't say anything about it because she knew what he was going through. As a nurse, she'd seen it more times than she wanted.

"I need to pray again," Rico said after holding her hand for several seconds. Chloe didn't bow her head or close her eyes because of the level of shock she was in. It wasn't that she didn't take prayer seriously, but watching and listening to the man Rico had become, praying and quoting Scripture, left her amazed. *Surely God is real if He can change my husband like this.*

Rico reminded God of his newfound faithfulness, his recent fasting and his belief that God could heal him. He even tried bargaining with God by promising to be even more devout if God would do this one thing for him. "You don't know how grateful I am that you are by my side. Even if I'm not completely cancer free, the Lord has answered one of my prayers. That prayer was to bring you back to me. I love you so much, sweetheart, and know that nothing will ever change that. I promise." Rico lifted her fingers to his lips and caressed them with three kisses, murmuring

"I love you" after each one. "This is it," he said after releasing her hand and reaching for the door handle to get out of the car.

Though they were in the parking garage, cooler than normal temperatures still washed over them as they made their way inside. Chloe pulled her jacket closer to her body as Rico threw his frail arm around her to provide his warmth, no matter how much or how little that did to shield her from the cool temperatures. That gesture did more for his heart than it did to warm her. The fact that she even allowed him to put his arm around her spoke volumes to him. Her body didn't stiffen and she didn't find a reason to wiggle out of his grasp, so that was progress and gave him hope that she heard him when he poured his heart out during dinner and maybe, just maybe, she was considering giving their marriage another try.

Both of them were caught up in their own thoughts as they walked briskly to the elevators. If Rico was now cancer free, Chloe would have to decide whether or not she would stay. Originally she was only going to stay until his chemo treatments were over and he got better. What was she going to do now if he was better? But then there was the side of this that she didn't want to think about. What if he wasn't cancer free? Was she going to stay until the end? She couldn't leave him to die alone. But miracles happen all the time. It was very much possible that he could still be healed. Was she to continue to put her life on hold? *Or make Shane wait for me?* She wondered. She hadn't thought about Shane much over the last couple of weeks, but she did miss him. She surprised herself by thinking of him in that moment. She hadn't spoken with him since she told him she wasn't returning immediately to Nashville. Regardless of whether anything was to become of her and Shane, she couldn't let that sway her decision in any way. She couldn't think about Shane right now. Her focus had to be on Rico, her marriage and their future—whatever it held.

∞

The cancer had spread throughout Rico's body. That was not the news he was expecting to hear at his appointment following his last round of chemo. A chill made its way through Rico's body although his temperature was rising. Chloe had remained by his side ever since she learned about the killer disease that was attacking his body. And today was no different as she sat next to him in the ice-cold doctor's office holding his wet palm. Her grip tightened as the oncologist delivered the news.

"So how long do I have?" Rico asked, fighting back tears. His face looked as if it were made of stone.

"Rico!" Chloe exclaimed, but Rico held up his hand to halt whatever she was about to say.

"So what's the verdict, Doc? Six months, three months, one month? What is it?" Rico pushed, becoming angrier by the second.

He'd spent the last several months growing closer to God, praying, reading his Bible, and doing right by his wife and yet he felt like God had shown him no mercy.

"Rico! Stop it!" Chloe chided. Even though it was very possible, she didn't want to think about him dying or talk about it.

"Let's get real. . . . I've gone through chemo and it didn't help. Isn't that what's next? Death? C'mon Doc!" Rico nearly screamed, his voice raised an octave higher as he became angrier. He wasn't sure if he was more angry with the diagnosis and knowing what it meant or with God for not answering his prayers the way he wanted. He knew God had the power to change his situation, but he'd already promised God that if his cancer didn't go away, he would still praise Him. He would still honor God and trust in Him.

The oncologist stood from his seat and walked around to lean against his desk. This was the worst part of his job—when his patients didn't receive the miracle they were expecting. Rico's cancer was already in an advanced stage when they caught it, and the doctor warned him that the chemo would likely not give him the outcome he expected. But none of that stopped Rico from trying. He had to try. He was turning his life around and he wanted to show God and his wife that he could and would be different, much better than before.

"About one month," the doctor finally replied with a sigh. Each time he had to deliver that type of news he wanted to cry as well but he couldn't. That was part of his job. He'd even prayed for Rico and would continue to pray. Faith was a part of why he chose this profession. He wanted to be God's hands here on earth, to help heal, to be a part of the solution.

Rico thanked the doctor for his time, beckoned Chloe to join him and walked out of the doctor's office. If he didn't have much time left, the last thing he wanted to do was spend his final few weeks sulking and feeling sorry for himself.

Not only was he not cancer free, the cancer had spread. He decided that he wouldn't let that have an effect on his faith; he would trust God until the very end. And even if his situation didn't change, he wanted to be remembered as a man who had faith—not the man he used to be.

Chloe trailed two steps behind Rico, trying to think of how she could comfort him. Being a nurse should have prepared her for moments like these, but it was quite different having to deal with a sick person who was her husband.

She caught up to him and took hold of his hand. When he took a left when they should have gone right to exit to the parking garage, she stopped, but he said nothing and tugged at her hand to follow him. When they had gone through the maze of hallways, Rico led them to the hospital's chapel.

Rico walked inside and knelt at a bench. She hadn't seen his face before now, but now that she could, her chest stung with pain. His cheeks were soaked with tears that continuously flowed from his eyes. Still with no words between them, Chloe knelt down beside him and rubbed her hand along his back. She felt him shake uncontrollably as he sobbed and prayed.

Chloe's heart tore into pieces at the words of Rico's prayers. Rico thanked God for the time God allowed him to have and continued to praise Him just for who He was in his life. Rico went down a laundry list of reasons why he was thankful to God for even preserving his life thus far. The humble man who knelt next to her, where did he come from? Where had he been? But it was no time for any of that now; it was time to enjoy what they had left. Maybe, just maybe, God would give them longer than the doctor had just estimated.

CHAPTER 33

It had been nearly a year since Chloe had awakened next to Rico in bed, and not only next to him, but curled up in his arms. Who knew when the last time would come when she would be able to do that? Just a couple of months ago, she was divorcing him, but now it was looking like death would do them part. And that thought kept her from closing her eyes.

She had been awake for at least a couple of hours, but she just couldn't bring herself to pull out of his arms. Even after feeling him stir, she dared not let go. The mere fact that he moved brought joy to her heart. She wanted to be close and remember how his body felt against hers. She wanted to remember all the good times they had together instead of everything that threatened to tear them apart.

"Good morning," he whispered, stretching but not releasing his hold on her either. He hated that it had to come to this, but he was sure glad that his last moments were going to be spent with her by his side.

"Good morning to you." She thought of asking him what he wanted to do today, but that had too much finality to it. She didn't want to think about him leaving this earth and she didn't want him to think that was on her mind either.

"I love you, Chloe," Rico confessed. There was no way he was leaving the earth without her knowing how much he cared for her. No matter what they had gone through in the past, right now, she was all that mattered and he planned to spend his dying days showing her.

"I know," she said, choking back tears. She held her position, not even moving to get into a comfortable position, which is what she would have normally done. Today she would endure the pain and get a massage later to knock out the ache that was sure to be there.

They spent a few hours in bed laughing and talking about many of the fun times they shared. Rico wanted to focus on the positive. If he even felt like their conversation was about to go down the path of his health, he switched the subject again.

He wasn't gone yet and vowed to spend some time showing her what she meant to him. He convinced her to get dressed so that they could go out and enjoy themselves, doing anything other than lying in bed all day trying to avoid the obvious, pretending as if the doctor's report didn't force them to face their mortality.

"I could go for some pizza, Little Caesar's hot and ready deep dish pizza."

"You do know that it's not even noon," Chloe reminded him.

Rico pulled his black T-shirt over his head, grabbed his watch from the nightstand and tightened it around his wrist. "Well it's two minutes after eleven, so that means it's lunchtime. Are you with me?" He wasn't in the best shape, but chose to pull himself together and push through his discomfort. He would suffer through those aches and pains; he refused to spend whatever time he had left living like he was already dead. Besides, God had the final say and he was still holding out hope that God would say something different and allow him a little more time on earth to spend with his wife.

"Of course," Chloe answered and slung her crossbody purse over her shoulder. After arriving, they parked on the opposite end of the parking lot, and walked hand in hand to the restaurant, as if walking a greater distance would extend their time together.

"Had we spent this much time together before, would our marriage be in a better place?" Rico wondered aloud.

"Maybe."

Rico thought about the R.A.S.P. meeting where the pastor asked them to find out what made their wives feel loved. He never did find out the answer.

"Let me ask you something. What makes you feel loved by me?"

Chloe looked up at him and turned her attention to the open parking lot in front of them. That was something she hadn't really thought much about in the past, and she wondered why Rico was bringing it up now. But instead of questioning why he asked, she thought about it for a moment.

"Transparency."

"What do you mean by that?"

"You trusting in us enough to truly be yourself, because when you were being open with me, I had your love, respect, and trust. I had all of you. And that's all I ever wanted." Chloe found over the years that when Rico showed his vulnerability, he was often humble and had no problem showing parts of himself to her that he would be uncomfortable showing to anyone else. The idea that he trusted her to hold his secrets and be his confidant made her feel loved. She'd always valued that closeness that made her feel their bond was unbreakable when he was transparent and honest. It was never about material things, and in her mind, there was no material item that he could give her that would substitute him sharing himself completely with her—mind, body and soul.

It was in that moment that Rico realized that if he had continued to be open and honest with Chloe, giving her what she desired most, his affairs likely would not have happened and their marriage would have indeed been in a better place.

∞

Chloe was truly enjoying the time with her husband as they strolled through the park in the crisp November weather, but became saddened when she thought about the holidays approaching. She started to wonder, *What if he doesn't make it to the holiday season? What if it happened on one of the holidays?* Squeezing her eyes tight, she shook her head to check herself and mumbled a curse for allowing her thoughts to travel down that path. *We have to have faith,* she chastised her thoughts.

"What do you think of having Thanksgiving dinner at our house this year and inviting our families?" Chloe suggested.

"I must be dying, because you just invited Diane to come to our house?" He chuckled at the thought, remembering the last time she and Diane were in the same room. He thought the nurse was going to have to call the cops to keep them from killing each other.

He paused his stride and turned to give her a peck on the lips. He slipped his hands into his pockets, rocking back and forth on his heels, admiring her beauty.

"Will I need to worry about you and Diane battling it out in the kitchen? You know she's a caterer, so she's going to want to do things her way, right?"

Chloe cringed at the thought. Rico was absolutely right. Everything had to be done Diane's way, but she would work to find some sort of compromise with her sister-in-law. Caterer or not, she hated Diane's food, so Diane could not be the only one in the kitchen.

"We'll all pitch in some sort of way. How does that sound?" Chloe responded after thinking for a moment.

"As long as you have a plan. I plan to watch football all day, not break up any catfights. But you're the level-headed one. I have no doubt in my mind that if something does break off, you'll be the bigger person," Rico said and winked.

"Umm hmm." Chloe playfully rolled her eyes and pulled one of his hands from his pocket to link it with hers so they could continue their walk. She was grateful that she didn't bring a jacket because the weather was exceptionally warm for mid-November, even in Houston.

Chloe ran her menu choices by Rico. She hardly ever got a chance to cook during the holidays because of her hectic work schedule, and the chance to do so now excited her in spite of the circumstances. She didn't trust Rico enough to leave a turkey in the oven if she were on call. She'd learned her lesson after their first Thanksgiving together. She was called into work and he let the turkey burn, being so engrossed in Thanksgiving Day football. Before that day, she had only witnessed a crispy black turkey on TV. Never again. Things had to be perfect this year. Now there was no work holding her back; she could cook to her heart's content.

With both of their minds preoccupied with what would happen soon after Thanksgiving, if the doctor's estimate was correct, they walked in silence. Chloe was trying to remember the moment, etching everything into her mind, from the way her hand felt engulfed in his, the beat of his stride, how the sun shined down on them, how she had to walk two steps to match his one, and the way his cologne teased her senses.

Chloe was content being there with him, which was the first time in a very long time, long before his affairs. But she refused to allow her mind to go there until they were nearing a couple with three small children, a little boy and a set of twins who looked a lot like Raegan, his ex-mistress.

She'd hoped her vision was failing her but knew that to be a lie when Rico's stride slowed to a stop.

"We can turn around and go the other way if you want to," he said. Her eyes were already locked on the family, and he glanced from them back to her. *Why do I keep running into them here?* he wondered. *Raegan doesn't live anywhere near here. But who am I kidding, I don't know where she lives these days.*

Chloe took a deep breath and smiled, resuming her steps to show that she wasn't bothered by seeing them. They were about fifty feet away, but it was clear who the family was. Caleb and Raegan sat on a nearby bench, with Caleb's arm around Raegan. One child seemed to be entertained by his gardening skills, pulling grass out of the ground, and the twins were each strapped to Raegan and Caleb in baby carriers.

"How are you doing?" Chloe asked, surprising herself. More than a year ago, she wanted to strangle Raegan, but now she had no ill feelings toward her. At least not any that would propel her to launch forward and get into a boxing ring with her. "Your children are so cute."

"Thank you," Raegan and Caleb both answered hesitantly. Raegan and Caleb looked at each other, slightly confused. An awkward moment of silence passed between the couples as Rico and Chloe stood smiling at the children.

The feelings Rico had for Raegan weren't as strong as they were before, if they were even there at all. He was now content with his wife being by his side. Something stirred within him. Gratefulness. Love. Peace. He wasn't sure why, but he wanted them to know that all was well and he truly did wish the best for the two of them. He'd known Caleb loved Raegan the moment he saw them together the first time. And Raegan was a good woman. He was glad that she got the love she deserved.

"I hope you guys can forgive me." Rico looked from the couple back to his wife. "I pray that God blesses you even more than He already has. You two deserve it."

"Thanks. We have forgiven you," Raegan said, and Caleb nodded in agreement.

"Good. Thank you. Enjoy your day. God bless you," Rico said as he and Chloe waved and continued their stroll through the park.

"I'm proud of you," Rico said to Chloe after they had walked away.

"Thanks but why?"

"You could have handled that in a totally different manner but you didn't. You were forgiving and classy."

"So were you."

Rico unlinked his hand and slid his arm around her waist. Even though Raegan's e-mail said that they forgave him, he felt a sense of relief and peace seeing her face again. Now he knew that she truly did forgive him for his wrongs against her. Her eyes were soft, much like they were when he first met her. But this time they glowed; he could tell she was in love with her family and the life she currently had. That gave him peace.

He told Chloe about the e-mail he'd sent to Raegan and how he'd tried to right his wrongs against her as well by asking for her forgiveness. Chloe had to know that he attempted to right his wrongs with everyone. He couldn't go to his final resting place knowing that people were still hating him.

"In that case, I'm proud of you too." She stopped for a moment to stand on tiptoe and plant a kiss on his cheek.

CHAPTER 34

To keep her mind off Rico's health, Chloe decorated their home for Thanksgiving, which she hadn't done in the past. From the sidewalk leading up to their front door, the yard décor screamed harvest season. Scarecrows and leaf-shaped solar lights led up the path and a thorny wreath adorned with orange and cocoa colored leaves and ribbons hung on their front door. The cherry oak kitchen table, arranged to seat about twelve people, was covered with a red, orange and brown tablecloth. The centerpiece was a glass bowl filled with fresh fruit and jumbo peppermint sticks, a tradition that her mother started during the holiday season when she was a child. Before their family arrived, she stood in the kitchen to admire her work and snapped a few pictures with her phone. She knew the space would look nothing like it did now after their folks made themselves at home; and in her mind, it could go on the cover of a magazine.

As planned, Rico sat on the couch with his eyes glued to the TV, watching any football game that would air that day. When he'd made himself comfortable, the doorbell rang, signaling the arrival of their first guests. Though he would be happy to see everyone, possibly for the last time, he didn't have the strength or the desire to answer the door every time the doorbell rang.

"Kelly, kids, Mom, Dad, so good to see you all," Rico greeted each member of Chloe's family with a hug and a kiss to both of the women's cheeks and then kneeled down to hug his niece and nephew. Standing again, his father-in-law clasped his hand and pulled him in for a hug—one of the most endearing hugs he'd ever received from the man—and definitely warmer than the last time they saw each other.

"Same here! You're looking good these days," his mother-in-law commented, squeezing him just a few seconds too long. Tears were about to escape her eyes when her husband tapped her shoulder to remind her that Chloe didn't want anyone bringing up Rico's illness; they were all there to celebrate and have a good time. No sulking.

After Kelly greeted Rico, she strolled into the kitchen where Chloe was busy injecting her turkey with marinade and stuffing it with celery, onions, and bell peppers. Kelly shimmied her shoulders, a goofy grin on her face as she got closer to her sister.

"God does answer prayers. You know that, right?" Kelly squeezed Chloe's shoulders and planted a kiss on her left cheek before backing out of the way to allow Chloe to work her magic on the turkey. "Maybe not always in the way we would like, but He does. My prayer for you through all of this has always been that you find peace. You seem to be at peace and I'm thankful for that."

"I am at peace. It's chaotic, but I know that things will work out as they should," said Chloe as she leaned back to accept her sister's embrace. She didn't have the heart to tell Rico or anyone else that their divorce became final a few days before. When she received the certificate in the mail, she stashed it away in her drawer. She'd already made up her mind to keep her wedding vows, whether that meant through *sickness* or *'til death do them part* –a sheet of paper wasn't going to stop that.

"They will. I'll keep praying. You know that, right?" Although she wished the circumstances were different, she was glad that Chloe loved Rico enough to stick around and make sure that he was taken care of after everything they'd gone through.

"Maybe next time we ought to have someone else pray. You weren't specific enough," Chloe half-joked. For the first time in a while, she was happy with Rico, but it sucked that she was happy now that they were legally divorced and his life was likely about to come to an end.

"We weren't going to talk about that, remember? So what can I help with? You already have it smelling good in here, girl," Kelly asked as she lifted pot lids and opened the oven door to check out the rest of the menu.

"You can wrap the ham in foil."

"Is that all, huh? If I didn't know any better, I'd think you were trying to say that I'm a bad cook."

"It's not that; I promised Rico that I would share the kitchen with Diane. You know how she is with her being a 'caterer' and all," Chloe emphasized using air quotes. Chloe must have summoned her with that comment because the doorbell rang as soon as the words slipped from her lips.

Despite the showdown in the hospital with Diane, Chloe would not allow Diane to ruin the holidays for her. She walked into the family room and greeted Diane, the rest of the sisters and their mom, hugging and planting a kiss on each person's cheek. Although her issues with Diane hadn't been resolved, today was not the day to deal with them. There would be peace in her home and she wouldn't hesitate to send anyone out of the door who threatened that notion.

"It's good to see you ladies," Chloe remarked as she pulled away from her mother-in-law's embrace.

Diane commented under her breath and rolled her eyes as she stood with her arms folded. She didn't believe the front Chloe was putting up one bit, but a glare from her sisters and Rico put her in her place. No one was having it today, so she had no choice but to back down, though she walked into the house with her defenses up.

"Diane, wanna come help me in the kitchen?" Chloe asked over her shoulder as she left the family room and headed back into the kitchen.

Diane followed her but didn't respond. As she entered the kitchen she mumbled something under her breath about all the decorations on the table.

"How are we supposed to eat with all of this stuff on the table?"

There she goes. Give me some strength, Lord. Chloe's back was turned to Diane as she rolled her eyes heavenward. She bit her bottom lip and ignored Diane's comment about the decorations. She attempted to divert Diane's attention to the food.

"I know you like making sweet potato pies. I have everything you need for that. I also left the dressing for you to make. The turkey and ham are both in the oven."

"Umph, figures. You don't know a thing about baking do you? Premade dough?" Diane sneered, pulling a box of rolled dough out of the fridge. "I don't see my secret ingredient either, so how can you possibly have everything I need in this tiny excuse for a kitchen?" Diane continued to complain.

Chloe slammed the knife down on the cutting board in frustration, nearly cutting herself.

"Look here. You and your secret ingredient can go to hell!" Chloe spat through clenched teeth. "If you don't see what you need, walk to the store and get it. It's as simple as that." Chloe plastered a fake smile across her face and turned around to continue cutting apples for her apple pie.

Diane pursed her lips and wrinkled her nose, but didn't say anything more after seeing that Chloe was probably on the verge of putting her out again. She would let her have it another day; besides, she was there to spend time with her brother. Her disgust for his wife could be contained for the holiday, at least. Every now and again, Diane would scrunch up her nose in Chloe's direction as if she smelled something foul, but she said nothing else out of line. For the most part, they worked silently in the kitchen for hours, baking, chopping, dicing, stirring and mixing. There were a few moments in between when Chloe asked about their trip to Houston or when Diane told childhood stories about Rico, but nothing about their strained relationship.

Turning off the burners and taking the dressing out of the oven, Diane walked into the family room, where everyone seemed to be watching Rico watch football, to tell them that dinner was ready to be served. As though none of them had had a bite to eat all day, they nearly raced into the kitchen to dig into Thanksgiving dinner. Rico leaned against the frame of the doorway, arms folded, with a silly grin on his face. Why hadn't they all been so loving before? None of that mattered now, but he was sure glad that he got a chance to witness peace.

Chloe glanced over to Rico from where she stood near the stove, proud of her dishes, identifying the sides and showing everyone where all the food was. After going over the menu, she walked over to him and wrapped her arms around his waist.

"Are you okay?" she inquired, nervously searching his eyes for the smallest hint that he didn't feel well.

Rico nodded, leaned forward and planted a long, soft kiss against her lips. If she had any doubt about his well-being a few moments ago, they were gone now.

"Yeah, you're good." Chloe answered her own question.

She turned around so that her head rested against his chest as they watched their families pile food on their plates and take their seats at the table. Everyone paused to look at them, waiting for them take seats at the table. But the talking, laughing and joking ceased when everyone took a look at Rico. Knowing that this would be his last Thanksgiving caused his chest to constrict as his eyes welled with tears. He'd been trying not to think about it, but how could he not? Sure, they would all soon leave this earth, but none of them had a clock that they knew about hanging over their heads like he did. For all he knew, this could be his last day.

CHAPTER 35

Though the table was large enough to seat everyone, elbow room was limited. The dining table was much too large for that space but Chloe purchased it just for the occasion so that everyone would have a place to sit. Ordinarily this would have been a scenario where Diane, if no one else, would have complained, but today they were all just happy that everyone had the chance to spend the time together.

"Let us pray," Chloe said, inviting everyone to join hands. A prayer that was supposed to only ask God to bless their food shifted to a prayer for Rico, in which not only did Chloe pray, but everyone around the table added their prayers.

Although Rico didn't want their time together to turn into everyone thinking about his health, he was grateful for the prayers. Perhaps God would hear them and give him a miracle. He remembered reading the story of King Hezekiah being granted fifteen more years of life because God found favor with him. He was nowhere near as righteous as the Bible says that King Hezekiah was, but he would be just as grateful for any additional time on earth that God would grant him.

There was not a dry eye left in the room when the prayers were finished. Their food was not as warm either, but that didn't stop them from feasting on it after the Amens, hugs and kisses to Rico, who hadn't even touched his plate. The love in the room was so overwhelming that even he couldn't contain his tears.

"Thank y'all for your prayers but this is kinda bringing me down a little. No more sad stuff. I'd like to enjoy y'all while I'm still here. Tell me a funny story or something," he said and chuckled slightly, diverting their attention away from his pain.

Diane immediately jumped in, resuming the stories she'd started telling Chloe while they were working in the kitchen. Most of her stories were centered around times when Rico got into trouble as a child and ended up getting his butt spanked. There were even times when she'd gotten him into trouble on purpose, according to her. His other sisters chimed in with their own stories, but then, their momma had a story like no other—the story of when he was born.

Something about the presumed ending made her think about the beginning. That was one story that she would never forget—her water breaking in the grocery store and being rushed to the hospital just in time to give birth to him. Parts of her story called for laughter, but it ended in tears flowing from her eyes as she thought about the baby boy that she once nursed becoming the man who sat before her today.

Diane saw how emotional their mother was becoming, so she interjected, talking about recent comedy movies and funny situations she'd encountered with her clients. They could all see from a mile away where her mother's story was headed. Everyone in the room would be crying pretty soon.

Chloe stepped out of the room and came back with Taboo. They could bond and have fun over that game without things getting too serious. She handed her niece and nephew coloring books and crayons to keep them busy for a short while, so as not to have their faces glued to TV watching cartoons all day.

Diane and Kelly were both self-proclaimed champs at Taboo and immediately started trash talking when the game came out. After placing their plates in the dishwasher, they made a beeline for the living room to get comfortable, select teams and play the game. Rico was grateful for the change in atmosphere. His mother had him about to cry as well. In fact, he always wanted to cry when he heard the story of how he was born, not because of the story, but because of the love and joy that he witnessed in his mother's eyes and voice every single time she told that story. He wanted to experience the same love and joy when Chloe birthed his children, but now it looked like he would never know what that felt like.

∞

Chloe and Rico lay in bed again, two days after Thanksgiving, just like they'd done for the past couple of weeks, entangled in each other's arms, neither wanting to move for fear it would be their last time being able to hold each other. Chloe noticed that Rico hadn't been eating much lately and his medicines didn't seem to be controlling his pain anymore. He'd become significantly weaker, needing help to and from the bathroom or to move from one room to the next.

Chloe was always the first to awaken, mostly because she could hardly sleep, so she spent most of that time praying and thinking. This morning was no different. Something didn't feel right though. With their families stashed away in the guest rooms, not far away from their bedroom, it was too quiet for a Saturday morning. She didn't hear the children laughing and playing, Diane fussing about anything or preparing breakfast, and she didn't feel Rico's chest heaving up and down. It was indeed quiet, but far from peaceful.

She stirred a little to see if Rico would tighten his grip or whisper "good morning," but there was nothing. For a few minutes, she fought the urge to check his pulse, thinking that his lack of response to her movement was all in her mind. After lying there for several more minutes, praying and hoping that he was just in a deep sleep, she lifted her head and peered at his face. His lips were curled into a smile but everything else about his face told her that the time had come.

Not wanting to believe that this had been the last time that she would lie in his arms, she resumed her position as her tears soaked through the T-shirt he was wearing. She prayed and prayed again, hoping that it was all in her mind or that she was having a bad dream. But not even the tear-soaked T-shirt caused him to stir. Still, there was no sound outside of their bedroom door. Maybe it was a dream.

She lifted her head to glance at the alarm clock sitting on the nightstand on Rico's side of the bed: 9:59 a.m. There was no way that every other person in that house was still asleep as well. It had to be a bad dream. She rested her head in the crook of his shoulder, between his chest and arm, squeezed her eyes tightly, prayed and willed herself again to wake up from this nightmare.

∞

The next few days were a blur for Chloe. She still couldn't believe that Rico died in his sleep, but she tried to find comfort in the fact that he was happy and he had renewed his faith in God. And not only that, she got a chance to witness it and experience him living his best life with his newfound spiritual maturity. Even though he hadn't always been that man, she was happy that he had become that man before going home to God.

She didn't know what she would have done without the support of both of their families. She could only thank God that they stayed around to help with the funeral and burial arrangements, calling family and friends and taking phone calls. They practically took care of everything; she didn't have the strength to do it.

She tried not to chastise herself for being away in Nashville when he first learned he was sick. There was no way she would have known since he didn't tell her, but that didn't stop her from feeling guilty.

Sitting on the front pew at church, nearly squeezing the life out of her mother-in-law and Kelly's hands, she willed strength from them to get through the ceremony. The hugs and the handshakes at the funeral and at the gravesite came through a fog. The only thoughts she had were *what am I to do now* and *what is next for me*. She'd originally put off moving back to Nashville, but now she was free to go there or stay in Houston. Neither of those felt like the right thing to do at the moment.

Back in their home, after the funeral, with all of their family with her, Chloe still felt alone. She peeled off her customary black dress, hat and heels and slipped into a pair of sweatpants and T-shirt. Dragging herself to the bed, she plopped down, hugged a pillow and released her anger, sadness and frustration.

A tap on her bedroom door interrupted her grief. Part of her wanted to ignore it, but knew she couldn't do so forever.

"Yes . . . what is it?" Her voice was faint as she tried to choke back her tears.

The door crept open and Diane peeped into the room. She was the last person Chloe expected to see and Diane knew it. And if she didn't, she probably would have known after seeing the confused look in Chloe's eyes. She'd hoped Diane didn't come to her room to start a fight about something she didn't like at her brother's services earlier that day. Chloe didn't have the energy or the will to fight with her.

"May I come in for a minute?" Diane asked. Kindness laced her voice, something that Chloe couldn't recall ever having received from her.

Chloe nodded and Diane walked into the room, closing the door behind her. Shocking both herself and Chloe, Diane uttered words Chloe thought she'd never hear coming from her mouth.

"I'm sorry Chloe . . . for everything."

Chloe still sat on the edge of the bed, squeezing a decorative pillow against her chest for comfort or to use it on Diane if she said anything out of line. Her eyes were wide with confusion. Diane's apology shocked her so, her tears stopped flowing.

When Chloe didn't respond, Diane continued, "I know I haven't been the best sister-in-law to you or treated you with the respect you deserve, and for that I am sorry. You don't have to forgive me today, but I hope that one day you will, okay? With Ricky being gone, it all seems so silly now."

Diane wrapped her arms around Chloe, who was still reluctant to move an inch. Diane sensed that Chloe was cold toward her and she didn't blame her. After releasing her, she walked back toward the door. As she was opening it, she heard the quiet word, "Okay."

Diane spun around, equally surprised at the new leaf they seemed to be turning over.

"I forgive you. Forgive me too." Chloe hadn't been as rude as Diane, but there were times when she could have handled things better. And she didn't know whether or not she may have unintentionally offended Diane, so she wanted to ask for forgiveness. She had no energy to hold on to grudges today either.

"Thank you. I don't need to forgive you. Anything you've said or done, I'm sure I provoked it. You know you were always the best thing that's ever happened to my brother, and for that, I'll always be thankful," Diane complimented before leaving the room and quietly closed the door behind her.

Chloe had no idea what had gotten into Diane. Maybe it was because they would no longer have any ties to each other and they probably wouldn't see each other again? Or maybe her brother's death had really given her a new perspective. She wondered what Diane would have done or said had she known that she and Rico were legally divorced already. She shrugged her shoulders and shook her head to rid herself of thoughts of Diane and her antics. No matter the cause for her wanting to make amends, Chloe wouldn't think about it too much; she would just be happy for the change in heart.

Chloe curled up in bed, still hugging that pillow to her chest, and allowed her heart and mind to think about the good times she shared with Rico, especially toward the end. She reached over and picked up their wedding picture from the nightstand and kissed his picture. "I love you, Rico. Thanks for finally giving me the best of you."

EPILOGUE

Every bulk item that Chloe didn't sell during the garage sales she had over the past two weekends was donated to Goodwill. She and Kelly sat around the now empty house taping up the last few boxes to be placed in the moving van waiting outside. The last six months hadn't been easy for her—from divorcing her husband to finding out about his cancer to his death. She had decided to move for good. She was now starting a chapter in her life that she'd never imagined she'd have to open.

Kelly had proved to be an anchor for her sister from the beginning. Even now, she did most of the packing, took care of the forwarding address for her, wrote thank-you notes to those who offered their condolences, and drove Chloe around town to take care of everything else. She'd hardly left Chloe's side for a moment. After the funeral, her children went back with their grandparents and she stayed behind with her sister.

Chloe had a few friends around Houston, but no one would be able to take the place of Kelly, who knew her best and loved her most. At the sound of the postman outside, Kelly put her packing task on hold and went to get the mail. Without looking through it, she handed it to Chloe and resumed taping the last box.

"Sure you're ready to come back home to us?" Kelly teased. Chloe hadn't lived in Nashville since she went away for college, so it would be a transition to live near her family again. She had enjoyed having them a plane ride away, but had grown fond of the idea of moving back home.

Chloe shrugged and smiled, fighting back tears. She shook her head as she thought about the new life that was waiting for her in Nashville. Sitting at the foot of the stairs, she flipped through the mail that Kelly had handed to her. Most of it was trash and she automatically began tossing pieces of mail to the side to be thrown into the recycle bin. Then she came across a familiar name in the top left-hand corner of a yellow envelope.

Any verbal response that she would have given to Kelly's question was halted when she saw Shane's name. She slowly ripped the side of the envelope and shook the contents into her hand. A neatly folded sheet of notebook paper slid out of the envelope. Before opening it, she glanced toward Kelly to see if she was watching. Thankfully, Kelly was busy taking a few boxes to the moving truck.

Chloe hadn't been in contact with Shane since she told him she was staying in Houston for a while, so to find a letter from him was surprising, yet refreshing and heart-warming. She hesitantly unfolded the letter and began reading. The sides of her lips curled into a smile as she read each handwritten word.

Chloe,

I can only imagine the pain you must be going through, but I want you to know that you're forever in my thoughts and prayers. As your friend, I'm only a phone call away if you ever need to pray, talk or just need a shoulder to cry on. No matter what did or didn't happen between us, don't let that interfere with you coming to me if you need me.

I'm still on light duty since the accident and things are going well. Don't worry, I'm taking my doctor and nurse's advice and taking things easy. So don't you worry about me. Make sure you take good care of yourself. And if I know Kelly, I'm sure she'll be doing all she can to help.

You are very blessed to have people in your corner who care for you and want to help you through this tough time. I just wanted to write to let you know that I'm one of them.

Shane

Chloe smiled and again fought the urge to cry, as she slid the letter back into the envelope.

"What's wrong?" Kelly asked, catching Chloe wiping at a tear that rolled down her cheeks.

"Nothing. I'm good," Chloe said and smiled. She picked up the rest of the mail and stood to take it to the recycle bin. She tucked the letter from Shane into her purse.

"Let's finish up so that we can hit the road," Chloe said, tapping her sister on the shoulder with the junk mail. She helped Kelly carry the rest of the boxes to the truck and returned inside the house one final time to look around. So much had happened there. She recalled the day she and Rico moved in and smiled. They were so happy to be starting their new life together, hoping to fill the home with lots of children, but that never happened. A wave of sadness threatened to overtake her, but she refused to let it. She'd promised herself that she wouldn't dwell on everything that went wrong but would remember everything that was right and look forward to her future.

She locked the door and placed the key in the lockbox. She'd decided to sell the house and start a new journey, one that she hoped would bring her a wealth of love and happiness with those who loved her most.

Book club questions

1. When Chloe returns to Nashville and is reacquainted with Shane, she meets him for lunch. Subsequently, she meets him at the Country Music Hall of Fame and for the July 4th outing. Even though she is now separated from Rico, do you think its okay for her to see Shane on multiple occasions? Why or why not?

2. Rico runs into Raegan at the park and notices that she is pregnant. A part of him wanted it to be his baby. Do you think that this was a sign that he wasn't over his relationship with her?

3. Shane knew from the beginning that Chloe was still legally married to Rico. Why do you think he continued to put his heart on the line knowing that there was a chance she could go back to her marriage? Do you think that Shane respected Chloe's marriage?

4. The word 'adultery' bothered Rico, although he knew that was the sin he committed. Much like Rico, many Christians are more bothered when biblical terms are used to describe their sin: fornication, adultery, gluttony, gossip, lying, etc. Why do you think this is an issue?

5. Chloe often thought or admitted that she couldn't get over Rico's indiscretions, but she left town to "think." It was

apparent, that her mind was already made up. Do you think she should have divorced Rico before she took a break and went to stay with her sister in Nashville? Why or why not?

6. Chloe sometimes held back her true thoughts and feelings toward Shane because she didn't want to be guilty of acting like Rico, but other times not. Is Chloe guilty of committing adultery as well?

7. Do you think Chloe's feelings for Shane played in a part in her filing for divorce?

8. Diane had always made her disapproval of Chloe very clear. Do you think Rico could have stood up more for his wife and marriage? What are some things you think he could have done to put Diane and the rest of his sisters in their place?

9. When Chloe found out about Rico's cancer, she decided that staying with him (even after receiving the divorce certificate) would fulfill her marriage vows. Do you think she was going above her call of duty or doing what she was obligated to do?

10. Rico felt compelled to seek forgiveness from both Raegan and Chloe. Do you think this was because of his illness or because he had developed a true relationship with God?

11. Do you think that Rico was only trying to build a relationship with God because of his illness? Why or Why not?

About the author

In addition to reading and writing, Natasha enjoys reading, cooking, couponing, and spending her time with her husband and children. She has won the Readers' Choice award for her books, _The Life Your Spirit Craves_, _Love, Lies & Consequences, and The Life Your Spirit Craves for Mommies_.

Natasha believes that we were all created for purpose and inspires women to pursue their God-given purpose through her books and the How Long Are You Going to Wait Conference. Sign up for her monthly newsletter at www.natashafrazier.com for encouraging devotionals, current events and new releases.

Connect with Natasha:

Instagram @author_natashafrazier

Facebook @craves.2012

Twitter @author_natashaf

e-mail: Natasha@natashafrazier.com

9 780988 452190